THE ENCYCLOPOCALYPSE OF LEGENDS AND LORE

Volume I

STEPHANIE ELLIS   ROSS JEFFERY   R J JOSEPH
RAYNE KING   BRENNAN LAFARO   TIM MEYER
MO MOSHATY   BRET NELSON
MOCHA PENNINGTON   STEPHANIE RABIG
JUDITH SONNET   MARKUS J WILLIAMS
KEN WINKLER

Edited by
JANINE PIPE

Encyclopocalypse Publications · encyclopocalypse.com

CONTENTS

INTRODUCTION

JANINE PIPE

I have always been fascinated by legends and lore. Growing up in the heart of Somerset, UK, not too far from Glastonbury, my childhood was filled with stories of King Arthur and The Green Man. Of Hanging Trees and Devil's Rocks. Vanishing carriages and even an actual flying pig thanks to my great-grandmother.

This childhood passion grew further into my teens with TV shows such as The X-Files only adding to the vast pool of creatures, cryptids and superstitions that I drew such enjoyment from. Ghostly Pirates at Jamaica Inn and the Beast of Bodmin Moor became bedfellows with the Jersey Devil, Sasquatch and Chupacara.

Over the years my intrigue for local legends has only grown deeper and thanks to the wealth of 'real' TV/YouTube shows and podcasts such as Lore, the embers of that fire have never burned out.

The idea to collate a bunch of stories inspired by such tales is not a new one but nevertheless something I was very excited for. Since this is the inaugural anthology from EP, I chose to invite some of the best and most diverse voices within the world of Indie Horror. Voices from varying backgrounds and with unique perspectives. My good friend and fellow author, Christian Francis, helped with this process and you'll find a selection of our colleagues within this First Volume. Alongside some more familiar characters, hopefully you'll discover one or two which are new to you.

Stephanie Ellis starts us off with a Norwegian treat. I adore Norse legends and this is a real feast for your senses. Steph proves it isn't just folk *horror* she's so adept at writing but folk*lore* as well.

Ross Jeffery delivers an excellent example of nastiness thus demonstrating one of many reasons why I invited him to be part of L&L. Ross is one of my favourite writers from the UK and after reading this, you just might agree. (TW = still birth)

R. J. Joseph broke my heart with her contribution. This story will haunt you, it may even upset you but is told for a reason. R J Joseph continues to be a much needed, hugely talented voice within indie horror and I intend to continue supporting her. (TW = child sexual abuse, rape, racism)

Rayne King proved he's a name to watch by writing his story within the space of a week. I threw down the gauntlet and he not only boldly accepted the challenge but blew it out of the gates. His tale of recklessness and unforeseen consequences also contains one of the best lines I have read in a short. You'll know it when you read it too - *chef's kiss*.

Brennan LeFaro shares a King-esque tale of childhood terror which wouldn't be out of place on an episode of Creepshow. I'm sure it won't be long before he shares a TOC with another New Englander with a love for the Red Sox. (TW - implied child abuse/neglect)

There was no way I was going to curate an anthology and not include the absolutely fantastic Tim Meyer. I've never read a piece of his work I didn't enjoy and this one was just as entertaining as everything else I've read and come to expect from Tim. He's a favourite author of mine for a reason.

Mo Moshaty warns us not to break traditions, especially regarding nature. I found this tale to be particularly creepy. Mother Earth isn't always benevolent and if anyone was going to bring that sense of dread, that feeling of your heart beating a little faster, it was going to be Mo.

Bret Nelson warns of deals with devils or in this case, losing your head to a witch's bargain Bret is a well-loved member of the EP family and it was a pleasure to showcase one of his short-form works.

Mocha Pennington is a voice I need more of and this twist on a well known fairytale is perfection as is usually the case with her stories. So long as I keep editing anthologies, Mocha will always have an invite. Her prose are something to behold and she is able to weave a story together like a beautiful yet devastating web. Finish this book then go look her up and read every word she has written.

Steph Rabig plays with a tale you may have heard before but gives it a face-lift and modern day setting which is just wonderful and totally believable. If you recognise the name of the character in the title, it won't give anything away. Steph is another voice I am here for and will support.

Judith Sonnet changes up what you should fear most at summer camp and believe me, Jason has nothing on what she has in store for us. For those more used to Judith's splatterpunk works in part owing to her love of Layman, this isn't quite in that vein, but you'll definitely appreciate the "Sonnetness" of this tale.

Markus Williams treats us to poems and a short love story between, well, I won't spoil it for you but this ain't no Mills and Boon.

And finally Ken Winkler proves there is more to fear than drowning and sharks at sea with a tale that would turn a pirate's hair white and your granny's cheeks rosey.

Each of these authors brought their A-Game and every contribution is the perfect length to flop down with in your favourite comfy chair with a cuppa or to read before bed. But if you get nightmares of axe-wielding squonks, spider monsters, or blood-sucking beasts, don't say I didn't warn you.

TRIGGER WARNINGS

Below is a list of Trigger Warnings for the stories we felt needed them.

The Womb is a Tomb = Stillbirth

Sad, Spooky Sally = Child sexual abuse, rape, forced pregnancy, racism

Reckless = Fatal car collision

Perchta = Implied child abuse/neglect

invitation to the
FEAST

STEPHANIE ELLIS

The road was empty, the sky the clearest blue. Snow-capped the mountains of the Oppdal valley, although the lower reaches remained swathed in the freshest green. Shutting out recent events, Hanna could pretend everything was normal; she was simply making her annual pilgrimage from London to her grandparents' remote cottage to recharge her batteries before returning to the relentless world of financial wheeling and dealing in which she operated. Except all that was fantasy.

She groaned as familiar nausea rose inside; the once longed-for baby had morphed into a vampire, leaching her of energy.

"Hey, we're almost there," said Mark, slipping his free arm around her shoulders and giving her a reassuring squeeze.

She gave a tired smile. Her husband had made no protest when she had suggested the journey, despite her condition. They had little alternative. Follow the general exodus into Europe where nobody knew where they were going or what they were doing, stay put and starve, or head to Norway and claim her inheritance. *A pity he wouldn't meet Farmor and Farfar*, she thought, although she was thankful her grandparents' end was simply old age and not the diseases running rampant across the world, resistant to any antibiotic.

The tiny village seemed deserted but occasionally she would catch sight of a shadow at a window. The few shops which had always done good business with tourists were closed. There were no broken windows, no signs of the looting and violence they had left behind. Hanna relaxed a little. Those who watched would recognise her.

The cottage came into view, nestled in the protective shadow of her uncle's white wooden church in whose grounds her grandparents now lay. She let out an audible sigh of relief. Their family had inhabited this dwelling for centuries, rebuilding when necessary, as walls crumbled and rafters sagged, refusing many an offer to buy from outsiders. Hanna recalled Forfar saying their ancestors had made a pact with Odin, one which he would uphold until he died—look after the land and it would look after you. The never-ending supply of vegetables and fruit from the kitchen garden and the clear spring water from a well behind the house was, he said, evidence of this. It was this memory of almost self-sufficiency which had driven them there. There was a chance. There was hope. To the side of the house, she caught a glimpse of the woodshed, the logs she had seen when she had attended their funeral, still there. Uncle Lars had said he would he keep the house ready for her return and it seemed he had kept his word.

"It's everything you said, babe." Mark eased the backpack from his shoulders and dumped it next to the wheelie suitcase.

She handed him the key whilst she freed herself of her own burden. The door opened into the cosy sitting room she had always loved, although the drawn curtains kept it shrouded in gloom.

"Let's get some light in here." Mark moved past her and was pulling back the curtains, opening the windows to air the room.

Hanna sat on the bench by the door and tugged off her boots, placing them next to her grandfather's shoes. Sorting through her grandparents' belongings was another task which awaited, something else Lars had said he would leave to her.

Mark started up the staircase, dragging their luggage behind him. He paused and looked at her, eyebrows raised.

"On the right." There was only one bedroom. When she visited, a small fold-up bed was put up in the tiny study.

Hanna wanted nothing more than to lie down and escape her punishing body but necessity kept her going. She took kindling from a nearby basket and set the fire ready for later. From what Farmor called the storm cupboard, she pulled out lanterns and candles.

"Well prepared," said Mark coming up behind her.

She laughed. "Farfar always one for just in case. A good thing considering how often the electricity went out. The generator's down in the cellar, we can look at that later." She pulled him by the arm to the kitchen door. "Come on, one more job before we can rest."

Hanna picked up some empty containers and pointed to the pump in the yard.

"All mod cons, eh?" said Mark, as the water slowly filled the container she had given him. He grinned at her, then his face softened. "Go on in. I'll sort this and join you in a bit."

Hanna kissed his cheek and made her way upstairs. She briefly considered her filthy state, her grumbling stomach, but exhaustion overrode everything and she flopped onto her grandmother's side of the bed and was soon sound asleep.

The sound of scratching woke her. At first she tried to ignore it, desperate to sink back into oblivion, to swim in the same darkness as her child. Then the whimpering began and Hanna reluctantly pushed back the blanket Mark had pulled over her and rose to her feet. Her husband didn't move and she saw no point in waking him for something so simple as a neighbour's dog. Except when she finally dragged her still-aching body downstairs and opened the door, she found herself welcoming an old friend.

"Rimny!"

Her grandparents' dog leapt up at her, tail wagging, slobbering tongue licking her face.

"Run away from Uncle Lars, have you? Knew I was home?"

She looked towards the minister's house but it lay in darkness. Rimny appeared well, although some of the weight he had carried had fallen away.

"You've been on a diet, eh? About time!"

She closed the door and he padded over to his old place in front of the unlit fire. The cold struck her for the first time and she quickly lit the prepared kindling.

"You can sleep here tonight. And then tomorrow we'll go and see Uncle Lars." The thought of seeing the old man warmed her as much as the flames which began to dance before her. She returned to bed with a lighter heart.

———

"I see we have a lodger," said Mark.

He was crouched over Rimny, fussing over the animal who was obviously enjoying the attention. She looked again, the poor dog seemed somewhat thinner than she recalled.

"No. A member of the family. This is Rimny, my grandparents' old dog. Uncle Lars took him in when they died."

"Made his way home then. Looks like he needs feeding up."

"Makes three of us," called Hanna, opening the kitchen cupboards in the faint hopes of finding something edible. To her surprise, tins and packets remained on shelves. *Uncle Lars, you treasure!*

"Seems Oppdal is not on anyone's radar." Mark had pulled out a couple of tins of soup. "I'll get these warmed up, think I can manage that."

Hanna continued to poke about. "Voilà!" She pulled out an odd tin of dog food in triumph. "We'll go and see Lars after we've all eaten."

"And washed."

She looked down at her dirt-encrusted clothes. "And changed."

It took a morning of heating enough water and filling an old tin tub to get themselves feeling human again. Their dirty clothes lay in a pile and Hanna had dug out clothes from her grandparents' wardrobes. She pulled on trousers, thankful Farmor believed in elasticated waists and a thick cable jumper which felt like an invisible hug from the dead woman. Mark fared almost as well although he had to cinch in his trousers and the jumper hung slightly loose.

Rimny spent the morning alternating between running

around outside and flopping down by the fire. He looked a lot better.

"Come on then," said Hanna. "Let's go and see Lars."

They made the short walk and found the door slightly ajar.

"Now we know how Rimny got out." Hanna knocked. "Uncle Lars! It's me, Hanna!"

There was no answer.

"Out tending his flock?"

Hanna shook her head. "He's getting on a bit. His flock come to him these days." She tried again. "Uncle Lars!"

Still no answer. She pushed the door wider and went inside. Rimny whimpered behind her and refused to follow. Her heart sank. She had lost so much of her family. Apart from Mark and herself, Lars was the last.

The house was cold, felt deserted. Sitting room, study, both empty. Kitchen. She took one look and fled outside, heaving the few contents of her stomach into the grass. Mark wasn't far behind.

"What the—" He was looking from her to the house and back.

"Explains why Rimny came home," said Hanna. "Why he looked so thin."

Mark frowned. "You don't think ..." He was looking at the dog, an uneasy expression on his face.

"No, I do not! Rimny's harmless. He would never hurt Lars."

"But if the man was dead and he was hungry. I mean his stomach—"

As Mark's voice trailed off, the image of the rotting corpse reared up. Lars' stomach had been ripped open, his guts looping out, hanging down. Had Rimny eaten him out of desperation? She headed back in, fighting back the tears as she did so. Much as she didn't want to go anywhere near the body, she had to take another look.

"Is there anyone round here we should tell?" Mark had

followed her in, although his intentions were already moving in a different direction. She wanted to scream at him to stop, to have some respect for her uncle. Survival, however, had no time for sentiment and so she bit her tongue, watched as he raided her uncle's food cupboards. It was necessary.

"Anders Andersen was the constable in Oppdal. We can go and look for him?"

Mark continued to empty the cupboard, ignored her comment. "He had quite a stash."

"The villagers looked after him."

"Well, something went wrong there then."

She nodded. Lars' head lolled against the back of the old wooden rocking chair he so loved. His arms hung over the sides.

A thought struck her. "There's no blood."

His clothes hung in shreds, revealing scraps of mottled flesh, remnants clinging to bones which continued to give him the shape of a human. His stomach, heart, liver, were heaped in a pile on his lap. Dull and grey and shrivelled. Teeth marks were evident in places. Rimny? No. The shape was wrong.

On a nearby table, a book lay open and she picked it up, thankful for the distraction. She recognised it. Lars had often visited their house when she stayed during childhood summers. He would appear and the family would sit around him as he read out tales from the Norse sagas, the old tales of Odin and the Aesir, the grim account of Ragnarök—not quite the end of the world but the end of the old world order. It was a story he had often dwelt on until her grandparents insisted he stop; he was scaring Hanna, they said.

His sermons, whilst steeped in the Bible, would often draw on these ancient tales. They were an apt metaphor, he said, for the current state of the world. She slipped the book into the old shopping bag on wheels alongside the cans and boxes Mark had already filled it with. Another bag, full of dog food was already stacked beside it.

"Come on," said Mark. "Let's get this home and then we'll go and see this Anders. And if there's no one there, we'll come back and give him a decent burial."

As they closed the door behind them to prevent any scavengers from entering and attacking the body further, another thought struck her. "He didn't smell!"

"Huh?"

"His body. It didn't smell."

Mark didn't answer and they continued their walk in silence, both preoccupied with the turn of events. Rimny brightened up the further away they got. She didn't blame him, felt the same way herself.

———

"Do you still want to go down to the village?" Mark stood in the open doorway, looking up at a glowering sky.

Hanna put the rest of the food away and joined him. She shivered as the breeze picked up in strength. "I think we should but if there's a storm coming, we need to make the house secure." She pointed up at the shutters.

By the time they had secured the wooden coverings, the sky had darkened further, the heavy grey turning morning into shades of night. The few birds she had heard were now silent. There was a pressure building in the air around her, inside her head. The coming storm was going to be bad.

Mark put his arms around her as they stared up the mountainside, battle-grey now, the clouds were sinking towards them, erasing the landscape beyond. The branches of the hawthorn tree at the bottom of the allotment stopped moving. Rimny whimpered and backed into the kitchen, his hackles up. The silence, the stillness was intense.

"Looks like Anders will have to wait," said Mark. "There's nothing we can do for Lars anyway."

He was right. Much as her heart ached at the thought of the old man's body continuing to rot in his chair, he could wait. Thunder rumbled. Closing the door behind them, they returned to the sitting room, lighting candles to alleviate the gloom and setting a small fire. With nothing else to do except sit out the storm, Hanna picked up Lars' book and began to reacquaint herself with the old tales.

"You'd love this, Mark," she said, coming to the story of the einherjar, the warriors in Valhalla and the Saehrimnir, the beast which was served as the main course for their feast. The latter would be brought back to life the next day and then served up again at the table to provide a never-ending meal. There was no reply. Both her husband and the dog were fast asleep on the sofa. She read on until her own eyes drooped. A loud crack of lightning, its shards piercing the dark room, made them all jump out of their stupor.

Mark rubbed his neck, groaning. "I feel as though I could do with a few more hours sleep."

"Make that *days*," said Hanna, putting the book down. "I'm going to crash out upstairs for a bit—if I can."

Mark rose with her, leaving the settee to Rimny.

A few hours later, the sound of whimpering again stirred her from sleep. Taking care not to wake Mark, she headed downstairs, annoyed and concerned in equal measure. A faint glow from the fire revealed Rimny's outline. He had shifted from the sofa to the hearth. His body twitched and he continued to whine but his eyes remained closed. She stroked his stomach and murmured his name, trying to soothe him with little effect. In the end, she couldn't bear his distress anymore. "Come on, old fella. Upstairs with me."

The dog shook himself and padded up the stairs, jumping onto the bed with surprising agility. Hanna tucked herself into the remaining space. She gave Rimny a final pat, noting the bones beneath his coat.

"Not much meat on you still, is there, boy? We'll have to change that."

Rimny thumped his tail in response.

———

"Ugh." A wet tongue was licking her face. Rimny's big brown eyes were staring at her. "What d'you want?"

He jumped off the bed and padded to the door, looking back expectantly. She noticed Mark was not on his side of the bed. Up and down, up and down, always her traipsing after the dog, she could barely contain her frustration. Why couldn't Mark help out?

The dog bolted down the stairs to the kitchen door and she let him out before going to check on Mark. She had spotted his body curled up on the hearth where Rimny had been. Obviously, it was the warmest spot in the house. He had brought a blanket and pillow down with him and looked almost comfortable except his body twitched and he was whimpering, very much as Rimny had done.

The sound of scratching at the door drew her back to the kitchen. She let the dog back in, lashed by rain as she struggled against the door in the howling wind; the storm had truly settled in for the night. Rimny skirted Mark and ran back upstairs.

Hanna knelt beside her husband and laid her hand on his shoulder. He groaned as if she had hit him.

"Mark, Mark." She kept her voice low. Whatever was causing her husband distress, she didn't want to add to it.

He didn't respond. She raised her voice, shook him harder.

He sat bolt upright, his face bathed in sweat, his body shaking. He looked around, eyes wild, not appearing to recognise her.

"Mark!"

He finally registered her presence. "Nightmare." His voice wobbled. "Horrible. Dreamed I was being eaten alive."

She had never heard him sound like this, so vulnerable, so scared. She pulled him into her arms and rocked him gently until his shaking eased. He felt frail, skin and bone. How had she not noticed his decline?

"Must've been seeing Lars like we did. Come on, upstairs."

Mark allowed her to lead him back to bed where Rimny was already settled.

"Just enough room for us," he muttered, but made no effort to push the dog away.

Hanna curled up under her side of the quilt, her worry over Mark not enough to keep her awake. The storm showed no sign of abating and the weeks of walking and living on their wits as they escaped from the UK had taken a heavy toll on their bodies. With shelter, food, water and warmth, came a renewed sense of security so they let their guards down and slept. The next day was a repetition of the first.

"Should've brought Rimny up with us," grumbled Mark, as the dog's whimpering woke them both again.

"Don't want him getting into the habit," said Hanna, reluctantly leaving the warmth of her blankets to fetch Rimny, who was soon settled between the couple once more. As she stroked him, she pondered how he could feel no more than rag and bones downstairs but seemed fine as he lay by her side. Her eyes closed only to be absorbed into a nightmare. Hands were grabbing at her, ripping her open, gouging out chunks of flesh which she saw devoured by hungry mouths. The sound of her own scream woke her. Rimny still slept peacefully but Mark had obviously given up the ghost and had ceded his side of the bed to the dog.

Hanna didn't want to get up again but was unable to sleep. The skies were still rumbling around them, the shutters rattling beneath the assault of the wind. Fumbling with a match, she lit the small oil-filled lantern on the bedside, wrapped another blanket around her shoulders and picked up the minister's book.

It fell open at the pages he had last been reading. A favourite tale? As she read, her Norwegian only slightly rusty, the pages transported her from their humble cottage to Valhalla. An etching showed an animal, its shape undefined in the middle of a huge table. Warriors surrounded it, some skewering its meat on their knives, others plunged hands into the cavity of the carcass, tearing out meat and offal, more were shown eating and chewing. There was an energy, almost a frenzy, in their act of devourment.

My nightmare, thought Hanna, turning away from the image with some relief, to the words which told the story of the feast of the warriors. Ragnarök, the end of the time of the Gods was almost upon them. As the wind brought the snow of Fimbulwinter and the wolves, Skoll and Hati, caught the sun and the moon, the warriors prepared themselves. The Saehrimnir, an animal fated to be killed and eaten, again and again, night after night, in a cycle of never-ending suffering—or at least until Odin's men, the einherjar—were summoned by him into battle against Fenrir's host.

Her eyes reluctantly shifted back to the illustration, it reminded her of how Lars had appeared—ripped open, devoured.

"Didn't come back to life though, did you?" she murmured. "A blessing, I should think."

She stifled a yawn and closed the book, snuggling down beneath the quilt. The wind had picked up again and it felt as if the temperature had dropped several degrees. She fell asleep longing for the storm to end.

Day and night felt as if they had merged. When she rose the next day, she had no idea of the time. Light trickled in through the slats in the shutters, faint lines carrying a strange tinge. Hanna's heart sank. The snows had arrived. She dressed quickly and dashed down to the kitchen, opening the back door. Snow piled up against the house, already as high as her waist, the handle of the nearby pump only just visible. They would have to clear a path to the pump —and the well—make sure they hadn't frozen. Spirits sinking, she closed the door and put some more wood on the range, the antique cooker and the fire in the sitting room were vital in keeping the house warm, and with the blanket of snow would have to work harder.

Putting a kettle over the open flame, she went to wake Mark. He had slept on the sofa this time, pulling it closer to the hearth. His eyes were still closed, his breathing laboured, his skin cold and clammy.

"Mark!" She shook him with no response. Placing her hand over his heart, she could only feel a faint murmur. She also felt something else, something warm and wet. When she withdrew her hand, it was covered in blood.

Frantically she pulled back the blankets. "Mark! Mark!" His clothes were ripped and cuts and scratches were carved into exposed skin. She stared, nonplussed. It looked as if he'd been attacked, but how? There were only three of them: Hanna, Mark —and Rimny. Rimny. No, it couldn't be him. He was old, teeth and nails worn down. And he had never hurt anyone.

Mark needed medical attention. When the snow eased, she would have to fetch the doctor. She didn't allow herself to consider there might be no medical support available. As she bathed her husband's wounds and applied the salves from Farmor's cupboard, she kept an ear cocked to the sound of the storm. She needed to be ready as soon as it eased. The day was spent nervously tending to the comatose Mark and keeping the fires going. Rimny kept her company but refused to go anywhere near her husband.

She pulled the old rocking chair closer to the fire, flipped through Lars' book again but every time it would fall open at the page of the feast. The sound of silence drew her back to the room. Hanna was aware of an absence. Mark's harsh breathing had stopped.

Unwillingly, she turned her head in his direction. She didn't want to look, sensing what it meant. But she wasn't prepared for the sight in front of her.

His blankets had been pulled back, clothes ripped away, his body carved open into a glistening mass.

"No, no, no." She rose but couldn't go near him. His body was a shell. Blood? There was no blood. Just like her uncle. Hanna picked up a blanket which lay at her feet and tossed it over him so that she wouldn't have to look at the mess of his body. She wanted to touch him, hold him, shake him awake but she couldn't. Instead, she just sat there, shocked, watching as the storm raged around them, the roar of the wind echoed by howling wolves.

How many hours she sat like that, she didn't know. It was a knock at the door which eventually roused her. She almost fainted when she opened the door to find Lars, standing whole and very much alive in front of her.

The world spun and it was only the firm grip of the minister which prevented her from falling, brought the truth of his presence home. Closing the door behind him, he guided her back in.

"Uncle ..." A thought struck her. If Lars had returned, did that mean her husband could as well? She couldn't take her eyes off him. It was a miracle. "Mark?"

"I'm sorry. There is no hope for him. Me? I was lucky." He sat down in her grandfather's chair, waving his hand for her to take her grandmother's seat opposite. "To be Saehrimnir is our curse and our honour and our duty."

Why was he talking about the stories now? Her husband needed medical help. "The Saehrimnir? That's just one of our old legends. And the creature is a boar!"

Lars gestured at the book which continued to flaunt its gruesome contents. "No. Nobody has ever been able to translate the word—and the boar—that was settled on as an acceptable answer. Our family, our village, has always known different."

Hanna remembered the shadows at the windows, the watchful eyes.

"In each generation, one is chosen and we suffer the agonies of being devoured night after night until either our hearts or minds give out. Until recently it was your grandfather. On his death, Rimny chose me ..."

At the sound of his name, the dog thumped his tail. Hanna frowned at him. She had always been told it was simply tradition that the family pet was always given the name.

"This animal was sent by the Gods," continued Lars. "He has been with us for centuries, choosing who should be invited to the feast. But I think Odin regarded me as a scrawny offering. Your arrival brought stronger meat."

She bridled. "Meat!" Mark was her best friend, her husband, the father of her unborn child.

"The Gods devour who they will. And is it not better that it should be your husband and not you? Would you want your child to go through the same ritual? Odin has been merciful."

Hanna stared at her uncle, the man who had lain eviscerated in his own home. "You expect me to believe all this?"

"How can you not when you see me and your husband?" Lars had risen and stood over Mark. "Look."

He pulled back the blanket and she forced herself to turn. The body appeared to be slowly healing, the flaps of skin knitting together, the tangle of viscera shrinking back into its cavity. Mark's eyes opened briefly and then closed again.

"Mark! He's alive!" She made to go to him but Lars stayed her.

"No. He needs to rest. And this world is already fading from him. Soon he will know nothing but the devouring."

No. Lars was talking rubbish. He was mad, that was it. And she was simply seeing things. There was something in the water. She allowed all these reasons to flood her thoughts and made another fruitless attempt to join her husband but Lars held her tight, rocking her as he had done when she was a child.

"You have to go," he said. "Leave him behind. If you stay, you might be next. So far, the Gods have spared you."

Hanna pulled back, angry, touched the dog collar at his neck. "How can you wear this?"

He smiled. "It is only a piece of cloth, the cross an adornment. Oppdal has always been faithful to the Old Gods—we have just had to hide it. Now that the wolves are howling and the snows have come, we no longer need to." As he spoke, he ripped the collar away and threw it into the fire.

"Ragnarök?" Hysterical laughter escaped her lips.

Lars took her hands in his. "Child, do you not remember the story? It is the end of the Gods and man will die—but not all. When it is done, man will emerge to begin again. The curse of our family has been the Saehrimnir. The blessing has been the promise that ultimately, we will survive. You and your child—the generations after, depending on how long the battle lasts—will be given the world anew."

"How do you know that for certain?"

"Because the knowledge of the gift has been passed down with the curse for centuries. If one is true, then so is the other. Now, the storm has eased and I can take you to Ulrich in the village. He and his family are leaving and they—and the Gods—will look after you."

"But Mark—" Again, she went to touch him, again she was stopped. Rimny growled in the corner. She watched in horror as his shape shimmered and changed, becoming a wolf. A hungry wolf. Terrified, Hanna allowed Lars to guide her to the door.

"He is beyond you, he is beyond us all. But I will come back after I have taken you to the village and remain with him."

Hanna shook her head, sobbing. "It is all my fault coming here."

"No," said Lars. "The Gods ordained this long ago. You had

no choice but soon, when they are done with each other—and with us—we will be free to follow our own path."

As they walked to the village, the only sound she heard was the howling of the wolves, a sound which would haunt her to the end of her days.

the

WOMB

is a tomb

ROSS JEFFERY

E lena was slouched behind the wheel of her car, the interior of which was bathed in darkness.

Scanning her surroundings, she quickly discovered she was hidden from the world; what she was about to do *would* go unnoticed for the time being at least, but the horrors she was about to unleash would, as always, be discovered in the coming dawn from the mouth of a screaming, hysterical mother.

The only light in the ocean of oily blackness which she currently presided, spilt into the car from the solitary streetlight in the centre of the somewhat abandoned hospital car park.

Her swollen, arthritic hands throttled the steering wheel as if it were a neck she was desperately trying to squeeze the air from. The leather creaked under the pressure she exuded, the skin of her knuckles morphing from a reddish aggravated pink to the bleached colour of bone the longer she bore down on the wheel.

Peering up through her open window, she took in the hospital: St. Maria Central.

She'd worked the graveyard shift in the maternity ward for the last six years, but after tonight, it would be time to move on, again.

She'd learnt throughout her lifetime that there was a threshold for stillbirths, an unknown and unspoken algorithm, which once triggered caused the powers that be to begin investigations and legal proceedings around malpractice and negligence of the hospital; and when their investigations turned up nothing, as it usually did, the bigwigs would soon turn their attention to the staff and she wouldn't wait around for that: because Elena knew she was as guilty as sin.

Relinquishing her grasp on the wheel she stared vacantly at her life-giving hands.

They were appendages which had pulled babies from their mother's wombs. Her deft fingers had unravelled the greyish-blue noose of an umbilical cord as it threatened to end a life before it had even begun; they were hands which had performed cardiac massage on fragile sacks of flesh and bone more times than she cared to count.

She'd brought many a life into the world, it was her job after all. But her calling, that was a different matter, because in answering that call, she'd taken a great many lives from the world too; and tonight, she'd be adding another one to her cull.

Life-giving hands. Life-taking hands. Semantics, really.

Elena glanced up at the many windows of the hospital.

This side of the building was the maternity ward and so she peered up and searched for her intended target – room sixty-four, Miss Harriet Braithwaite – as her fingers busied themselves with undoing her blouse in the privacy the darkness of night afforded her.

She'd managed to unfasten three buttons before her eyes finally alighted on the room, she paused.

Miss Braithwaite was a thirty-eight-year-old mother-to-be, with no husband in the picture to speak of. Her age was the sole reason Elena had singled her out for tonight's harvesting. She knew a stillborn in a mother of this age was not uncommon, if anything *geriatric pregnancies* were full of complications; the womb becoming a tomb was just one of them.

Elena's gnarled fingers continued to seek out her buttons as her eyes stared longingly at the open window. Her delicate, soft voice tumbled from her lips in a serenade, as it recounted the various complications which could accompany a geriatric pregnancy in her best bedside manner.

A sly, smile graced her lips, recalling a conversation one of the locum doctors had had with her two nights ago after she referred to Miss Braithwaite as a *'geriatric pregnancy'*. He'd informed Elena quite curtly that: *'We no longer call pregnant women over the age of thirty-five geriatric, we use the term* advanced maternal age. *You'd do well to remember that in the future Miss Laakko.'*

Elena didn't give a damn what the new terminology was, people were too scared of offending people nowadays, so instead they offered platitudes to placate this easily offended generation. Elena had always been bullish, stuck in the ways of old – she'd seen a great many more winters than the young buffoon of a locum – and so she'd call a spade a spade whenever she saw fit, regardless of who she'd offend in the process.

"Premature birth, low birth weight in the baby, chromosomal defects, labour complications, caesarean section…" Elena was salivating at the prospect of her reaping and the weeping which would follow in its wake, knowing each morn-filled cry; each grief-laden lament would form a delectable and diabolical symphony played solely for her ears.

She slurped the spittle back down before continuing her crazed ramblings.

"High blood pressure in the mother; which could lead to preeclampsia, and an early birth for the baby. Gestational diabetes; which also increases the risk of diabetes later in life…" and then she came to the sweetest of complications, becoming giddy with the utterance:

"Stillbirth."

She smiled, savouring every vowel and consonant as it trickled across her tongue.

Elena had finished unbuttoning her blouse and so she began slipping the blue fabric from her shoulders before tugging it free from behind her resting body, folding it neatly on her lap; once finished she placed it neatly on the passenger seat.

In her nakedness Elena's nipples hardened quickly from the cold air which stole through the window, the inquisitive fingers of the wind caressing her flesh with icy tendrils as if it were a lover's hand. She was braless, she had to be on the nights she'd make her harvest; the straps of her lingerie caged her in, restricted her movements – clipped her wings in a sense – when she needed to be free and mobile and above all else, quick.

Reclining in her seat, naked from the waist up, her eyes were quickly drawn back to the window as if the delicate meat of her eyes were filled with iron filings and the window – and more importantly –what lay beyond its glass was a magnet pulling her gaze ever-onwards. Her long, grey hair tousled down either side of her slender, wrinkled neck, spilling in a follicle shawl over her nakedness, concealing her breasts and protecting what little of her modesty remained.

It had been a long time since she'd last fed, and as Elena glanced down at her sallow skin, which appeared slack in previously firm places; she knew she couldn't last much longer without suckling. She'd grown too cautious of late, sacrificing her desires and needs to ensure she wouldn't be discovered or forced to move on from her fertile hunting grounds due to an investigation caused by her inability to stop her unquenchable thirst.

Her fingers were probing at her stomach, dancing over the rolls of slack skin, searching desperately for the silvery-pink thread which begged to be unwound. The tips of her fingers soon brushed against it, a raised prominence of knitted skin. Peering down revealed two liver-spotted hands, one gripping a handful of her bunched-up, sagging skin. The fingers of the other hand busied themselves in tracing the pink scar which emerged from her naval and ran horizontally towards her left hip; where it disappeared around her back before returning to her naval via the right hip, knitting together in a fleshy protrusion from her naval as if it were a malformed ear grown on the back of a mouse.

Her eyes darted to the dashboard, resting atop of it, glinting in the scant light was a scalpel.

Keeping her fingers on the scar with one hand, as not to lose her place in the dimness of the car's interior, Elena relinquished the folds of sagging flesh with the other and reached for the blade.

Shifting her slack skin again to obtain a better view of her incision point, she then placed the tip of the scalpel to the puckered, pink flesh and breathed deeply. The process was the same each time, and it reminded her of childbirth, sometimes the thing that was hidden inside, away from prying eyes, needed a helping hand to enter the world. As the point of the scalpel pricked her skin she mused about what she'd often say to the many women on her ward faced with a daunting task of a caesarean section: *'We're just going to be taking the baby out of the sunroof, there's nothing to fear, we'll have baby out in no time whatsoever.'*

Buoyed by the recollection, Elena didn't hesitate as she plunged the scalpel through the thick vine of scar tissue, dragging the snagging blade to her left hip; it was a practised routine and she delicately traced the whorl of flesh which bisected her body with surgical precision. She pulled the scalpel free at her side before plunging it back into her navel to slice through the scar tissue to the right. In her haste she winced as the scalpel bit too deeply into the widening wound, nicking her hip bone as it exited her side.

With her abdomen now split open – her body existing in two parts, above and below the bloodied line – Elena deposited the scalpel into the cup holder, she knew full well that the incisions she'd made would tear along the scar-tissue around her back when the time came for complete separation as if it were a zip in her flesh.

Blood sluiced from the wound as she fidgeted in position, washing everything beneath the crudely drawn line in a deep crimson, but in the meagre light afforded by the distant streetlight, the blood appeared almost black – a slow-moving tar – as it seeped from within and dribbled down into the dark, wetness of her crotch.

She quickly began fidgeting in her seat, but it wasn't from the pain, because there never was any pain. Her discomfort came from the ache which now spread across her shoulder blades, causing her great distress. It was a sting which begged unceasingly for Elena to scratch, to tear her flesh raw in an attempt to vanquish it from tormenting her. Each time it presented, on the nights she fed, it felt as if she was on withdrawal from heroin. It was a drug Elena knew the side effects of well, with users always battling the compulsion to scratch the itch which never truly resided in their skin in the first place, or one that would ever subside once they got a hankering for black tar. Immune systems quickly become compromised from excessive use of heroin and in turn, the body tries to rid itself of the harmful substances it ingested in any way possible. Nerve and neuron receptors in the skin beg for a release that will never come, each clogged up by the heroin which has already bonded itself to them like glue; leading to injection sites becoming scratched raw, faces clawed open to release an itch which doesn't preside under the surface, their broken skin quickly turns to a sea of abscesses and infections and sooner or later blood poisoning.

Over the years Elena had delivered her fair share of babies addicted to opioids; observed their tiny, fragile bodies wriggling and writhing like pupas within a chrysalis as they suffered the agony of withdrawal once separated from their mother who drip-fed them smack via their umbilical cord, a willing dealer to an unborn child.

The sight of those screaming children struggling through a hell not of their choosing was too much to bear and the grisly spectacle often spoiled Elena's appetite.

She learnt early on not to suckle from foetuses tainted by addiction – it was a fate worse than Hell itself.

Her hunger had once forced her to sup at a foetus contaminated by heroin – needs must when the Devil's driving – but the pain and suffering it caused her afterwards, was something she wouldn't wish on the worst of her enemies. Her teeth felt as if they were going to fall out, and some did, detaching themselves from her blistered and raw gums. But it was the pain which seeped into her bones that made her never suckle from a tainted foetus again. It was an ache so intense it felt as if someone had broken every bone in her body; each inhalation and exhalation made it feel as if her shattered ribs were plucking at the greyish-blue bags of her lungs, hands threatening to puncture those bags of air with beseeching talons of razor-sharp bone. She couldn't sleep, wouldn't sleep for six days; that was how long the tainted, poisoned blood stayed in her system. Each hour was torture and each passing day was endless suffering. So now she stayed clear. Elena had learnt her lesson.

Clean mothers and even cleaner children were the only meal on the menu.

Elena suddenly cried out in pain, her voice carrying into the parking lot as if she were a vixen being mounted; the shout echoed briefly in the night before the darkness smothered her wailing as if a pillow were being placed over a dying patient's mouth. Her screams; her petitions of sweet release still resounded in the car though, reminding her fleetingly of birthing mothers with crowning children. Their suffering. Her suffering. All mingling together in one giant symphony for the damned.

Her body thrashed forward, she gripped the steering wheel tightly; bore down, gritted her teeth. Veins and tendons announced themselves quickly in her neck like corded ropes as she strained against what came next: her birthing pains.

She opened her mouth and bit down on the steering wheel as the sound of fabric being torn announced itself to the night. But it wasn't her teeth which had found purchase in the leather which brought the sound to her ears, it was her skin splitting. The skin between her shoulder blades tore from the nape of her neck to the mid-lumbar as warm wetness trickled its way from the wound and dribbled down her back.

She fidgeted in her seat – something akin to a palsied fit – as her jaws remained clamped to the steering wheel; drool fell from between lips and leather in gloopy, translucent cables. Her body shivered as something began to unfurl from within. This part of her transformation always brought her close to fainting, as hidden appendages withdrew from their cramped hibernation, uncoiling themselves from within; wriggling free from the fleshy prison they'd been interned to for weeks and sometimes months.

With a shuddering fit and a final, muffled grunt of pain, Elena released her mouth from her temporary bridle bit; they were finally out. She panted like the many mothers she'd tended to previously, each exhausted after a protracted and difficult birthing, but also fascinated to see what all their pain and suffering had brought forth into this cruel world.

Elena turned her eyes up to the rear-view, marvelled once more at the gore-soaked majesty of her wings.

Her wings continued to unfurl behind her as if they were fern leaves emerging from the mulch they'd been gestating within; each wing slowly took form, curling and solidifying in place, membranous and sinewy appendages born into a dark night. They flapped briefly, blood splattered the inside of the car. Now free from their coating of gore, Elena could see clearly the skin of each wing, so thin and delicate they appeared almost translucent – as if they weren't there, glass-like – were it not for the black veins which decorated and snaked through their veil-like form, giving them size and shape and a growing wingspan.

The sight of her wings always reminded her of the placentas she'd have to pick through once baby – still breathing, but sometimes not – was finally reunited with smiling or grieving mother. It was more often than not her job to inspect the organ closely; a task she set about diligently with lithe fingers, a keen eye for detail and a salivating mouth. Being that close to what she craved most was euphoric. She'd often find herself weak at the knees as her hands sifted through the purplish blue and sometimes greying afterbirths. Even though she was often lightheaded, battling her debilitating yearnings, she was nothing but professional, to be anything less would cause suspicion, would force her to seek pastures new. So, Elena would sift and sort, ensuring firstly that the placentas hadn't fragmented, that what she was dealing with was a complete specimen; in doing so it meant that there were no risks of placenta accreta, which would bring on significant blood loss after delivery and the possibility of a hysterectomy.

Nothing spoiled her appetite more than the word *hysterectomy*; it was so finite.

For mothers, it meant no more babies – sad but they'd get over that with time – but for Elena it meant fewer opportunities to graze, fewer cattle to slaughter, one less field to reap and suckle from.

Suddenly, with the word *hysterectomy* lodged in her brain and about to cause an aneurysm followed by a paralysing ischemic stroke, Elena's wings began to beat furiously; they'd grown a mind of their own and had decided that now was the time for complete separation, they couldn't delay for another second because to do so would cause their meal to run the risk of being spoiled. Elena knew they were right, if she waited any longer, she may be forced to survive for another day or another week until the next opportunity presented itself. How long could she truly survive without the sustenance she craved? She didn't know the answer to that question, all she did know was that she was hungry and the time for thinking and plotting was over.

Her frantically beating wings soon stirred her into action and motion and she gave herself willingly to their calling; surrendering herself: mind, body and soul to their awaiting meal, reservation for one.

Her body began to rise. A gushing sound, similar to a shallow river rushing over a riverbed of stones began to emanate from her midsection as the scalpel line – drawn not moments before – widened around her torso. Insides soon moved to the outsides as they ran over and through a latticework of fringed flesh, torn abdominal wall and guts. The floodwaters which had been held back were suddenly released in a brackish wash of organic detritus and a vermillion-coloured soup which poured and pooled warmly into her lap, covering her now redundant legs.

The sudden emptying was quickly followed by the sharp, but always comforting snap of total separation as her torso detached and her wings carried her out of the window and into the night.

Her guts tumbled from within her as if she were a sack of potatoes being upended, long greying tubes of intestines fell from within, organs sluiced out, slapping wetly in the car, over the door or onto the blacktop as she made her way into the night. She glided closer to St. Maria Central, dragging her guts over the ground like a macabre wedding train, carving a bloodied path to her supper. As she approached the darkened wall of windows, behind each wall of glass a meal was waiting to be scoffed down, her eyes rose to the window of room sixty-four and where she would suckle from Miss Harriet Braithwaite's unborn child.

She rose higher into the night. She rose above her lowly circumstance. She rose with the need to feed. To reap from her dutiful harvest. Higher and higher her beating wings took her. Elena's hanging guts carved a gore-riddled streak up the wall, as if a giant leech, fit to bursting from a recent feed had scaled the outside of the building, looking for a place to bed down and enjoy their full and bloated stomach.

Her trailing innards squeaked against the darkened glass, but there was another sound which called out louder to her than that of her own ruin, it was a sound which beckoned her on. It was a gentle thrumming; subtle at first, but soon others joined in the call as she passed the numerous windows and ventured higher to her prize, turning into a deafening drum roll; a banshee cry made up of the hundreds of tiny hearts which beat in hundreds of tiny chests, trapped temporarily behind glass and inside burgeoning wombs: wombs, which Elena was determined to turn into tombs by the end of her supping.

As she neared room sixty-four, she paused, her wings beating manically, keeping her hovering in place like a hummingbird. Her eyes grew wide, ever observant in the moments before feeding because she had to be careful and silent, even when all she wanted to do was rush in and feast.

From beneath the bloodied, pendulous remains of her guts – which swayed in the air like the weight in a grandfather clock – something began to emerge from deep within her torso. Slowly an additional appendage wriggled free, jointed in three places and as thick as an arm at first; it slowly began to unfurl, reaching out from its place of redundancy and incubation, as if it were an arm that had been slept on and become deadened, detached momentarily from the whole being – a phantom limb.

It slid from between the curtain of membranous and gore-riddled guts, where it finally extended into the night unsheathed and ready for what came next.

Elena stared at her proboscis. The end glistened wetly in the sliver of moonlight which shone down on her, bathing the hideous scene before her in an aura of regality. She smiled at her monarchic reflection in the glass before her body shuddered with the tantalising gift of pain which would soon be birthed from behind the pane of glass which held her reflection. A loyal subject's unknown and unending gift of suffering would soon become her eternal offering to the goddess of the night; because Elena was a queen, not of this world but of the one in the shadows, the one made by lore and legend, she was something to be adored, to be revered, worshipped; and above all else, feared.

The proboscis stretched out before her, revealing itself in all its finery and majesty; the end was thinner than the shaft it emerged from, needle-like in its tip. The skin that sheathed her stinger continued to be drawn back, bunching up at its base in a veiny knot of flesh where she felt it throb rhythmically as it pumped poison – anaesthetic – towards the business end of her new organ.

The anaesthetic beaded on its tip, glistened in the moonlight for a brief moment, before trickling down its slender length, much-needed lubrication for what came next.

She moved through the open window and into the fertile grazing pastures that awaited her. Stealing stealthily into the room, the proboscis which reached out inquisitively before her continued to ooze more of its numbing fluid, which dribbled in silk-like ropes from its head, like a broken spider web caught in an autumnal breeze, dribbling its secretions across the floor in front of her. There was suddenly a wet slapping sound as Elena's guts followed her over the divide and tumbled to the floor like wet ropes thrown on the deck of a fishing vessel, splashing the ground in gore. Her flapping wings brought her to the end of the bed, their constant thrumming stirring the stale air of the room, lifting the subtle but tantalising bouquet of impending death to her nose. She smiled.

Her dutiful hands peeled down the blanket which covered the swollen, beached whale of a mother; the same arthritic hands began to slowly raise mother's gown, Elena's proboscis rose as if smelling the scent of food in the air, its sleek and syrupy covered tip hungering ever-onwards, extending slowly towards the rotund and stretch-mark-riddled stomach of sleeping mother and the child sleeping beneath its surface.

Elena reached out and cupped the mother's swollen stomach with her hands as the proboscis descended upon the stretched, taut skin. She felt the baby wriggle beneath the surface as if it were trying to hide, burrow deeper, away from the needle-like tip which fluttered around mother's stomach, tracking its prey beneath the skin with whips of dexterity, honing in on its incision point.

As the child relaxed and as its exhausted mother slept on, the proboscis began to tap at the surface of her skin, testing the roundness and the plumpness of the belly which was trapped between each of Elena's wisened hands; probing the mother's stomach as if it were a cantaloupe and Elena were casually testing it for ripeness in the aisle of a supermarket.

The head of the proboscis traced over the mother's stomach

as if it were a finger made up of many supple joints before it stopped suddenly in its loving caress. The skin which had bunched up below its needle-like head – pulled back like some hideous foreskin – began to throb, pumping even more anaesthetic to its shining tip. Fluid sluiced from within, coating the end once more before it dribbled down onto her exposed stomach. Elena shuddered as the tip began to descend, pushing into the mother's stomach, dimpling the skin; the taste of what was to come already making her salivate.

Soon she would taste what she craved most and it would be heavenly on her tongue.

The skin of the stomach gave way to the scalpel-like stinger. Mother moaned but remained asleep, the anaesthetic numbing her from the chest down, a cruel epidural where there would be no child waiting for her at the end, one that was alive that is, only a shoebox coffin and tiny, knitted burial clothes and an unending grief awaited Elena's prey. The unborn child, asleep or awake – it didn't matter to Elena – didn't move, it was tucked up tightly in its amniotic sack, trapped between Elena's vice-like grip as the proboscis slid deeper and deeper still. Burrowing closer and closer to sup at the nectar she craved most, the sap of a foetus which would not only scratch the itch she'd buried for far too long, but it would sustain her, give her sustenance for the long journey ahead; when she would arrive in another town, another hospital, ready to reap the harvest of the unborn which awaited her arrival.

With a final thrust, from her veiny, throbbing, desperately hungry appendage, the proboscis slid home, puncturing through the amniotic sack and lodging itself into the child's heart like an arrow loosed from a skilled archer finding its target, but with the deft brilliance of surgeon performing in-utero heart surgery, because the child needed to be alive during her feasting.

The proboscis throbbed once more.

Instead of pumping fluid to its poisonous tip, it now sucked, swallowed; drank the child dry from within its temporary, but now all but broken home.

Elena felt the child's lifeforce begin to fade, her meal beginning to be tainted by the bitter tang of death, as the child slowly succumbed to its withering. Without a conscious thought, as if her proboscis had grown sentient and, in a way, it had; always operating with its own agenda, its own diabolical desires, it began to slowly withdraw from child and then mother.

The tip emerged from the dimpled skin of the stomach as if it were a hypodermic needle, leaving no trace of its previous invasion and robbery; raiding this mother of all she had nurtured, brought to term and clung on to so steadfastly. There would be no birthing of life from between her legs, because all mother would birth now was death – which was Elena's gift to all her victims, one that could never be returned however much they hated it.

With her harvest made Elena fluttered towards and then out of the window, dragging her trawler's net of innards behind her. She slipped from room sixty-four and began to descend to her car, where she would reattach before finding the freedom of the open road as she searched for fertile hunting grounds further afield. But as she descended, with her last meal still coating her tongue, she became aware of the tiny, beating hearts behind the open windows she passed on her way down.

It was a maddening cannonade, one that didn't signal the end of her meal or the soon-to-be sudden departure from the life she'd manufactured for herself at St. Maria Central; it was a rallying cry, an invitation she could not turn down. She stopped her descent, hovered in the moonlight as her innards hung below her in gelatinous ropes of vermillion and caught the sight of her reflection in the glass; she appeared as an avenging angel from a Baroque painting, chiaroscuro in action, her flesh configured and reflected back at her in shadows and light. Slowly she turned her head up to the windows above her, her eyes seeking out the numerous open windows, each window contained a wriggling soul beneath a sheet of flesh and blood.

She smiled as her proboscis rose again; its stinger glistening in the moonlight, the tip already dribbling its aesthetic juice down its shaft; it, like her, was salivating at the prospect ahead, because the journey ahead of her would be a long one after all.

Instead of settling for a snack, which would tide her over for a day or two at the most, Elena glided over to the first of the many open windows, and she was ready to savour the exuberant banquet which had been laid out before her.

She would have her fill and by the morning she would be gone.

sad, spooky
SALLY

R J JOSEPH

"Mommy, Savvy went potty two times in her dipey." Three-year-old Tariq Smith made the admission in a tiny voice just above a whisper, hoping his Mommy heard him and came to help. His baby sister was only a year old and she whined a lot due to the broken rash that perpetually remained in her diaper area.

"Shut up all that damned noise!" Their mother bellowed from the other end of the apartment.

"But we hungry, too, Mommy." He clung to the door jamb with sticky, cold hands. Tears rolled down his chubby cheeks. Savanah's whimper revved up into a full-blown cry. Tariq held her hand and looked around the room for a fresh diaper. Savanah was more than half his size, but he thought he might be able to figure out how to put her diaper on, if he found one. He regularly changed his own diapers.

"Can't you make them be quiet?" Tariq didn't recognize the man's voice. He also couldn't tell if he was a nice man or not. He sounded mean and most of the visitors their mother had over were mean to them. Tariq had to assume that man would be mean to them, too. Mommy usually didn't let the men hit them—but whenever one of the men hit Mommy first, he always came to find them.

———

The pain searing the tender flesh of Sally's abdomen sliced sharper than the scythe she had just swung to cut the brush at her feet. She doubled over and tried to stop the overwhelming waves of nausea rushing over her. She had ignored the ever-increasing intensity of the cramps and kept her pace with the others around her, thinking if she pretended the baby was not coming then it simply would not be.

Tati Jane, the plantation's healing woman, had told her all about what to expect. She could only remember certain parts because at ten years old, she had no point of reference for much of the information. Also, having the knowledge—whether remembered or not—and going through the actual experience were different things.

She almost wished to feel the bite of the whip between her shoulder blades to take her focus from what was happening within her body. Sally was young but her stubbornness had already resulted in two lengthy sessions at the whipping post. The first time, she was punished because she had taken an extra biscuit from the house dinner table.

Tati Jane always ate so little and Sally thought a little bit of extra food might help the elderly woman get over the malaise she had currently been suffering. She never had the chance to see if it would have helped because David, the master's eldest son, had told on her and slapped the biscuit from her hands before smashing it into the hardwood of their kitchen floor.

He then spat on the ruined bread and punched her in her temple before grabbing her by her hair and dragging her into the sitting room where his father sat, waiting to hear about her transgression. Master ordered David to take her out and whip her, himself, so he could start asserting his dominance around the plantation. It had not mattered to them that she was but a child, so young her budding breasts had not yet bloomed.

It also had not mattered that she was too young to have even had her second monthly flux: she was not too young for David, and then Isiah, the master's younger son, to take turns hurting her down under her clothes after David whipped her. She had fought both men to try and keep them from violating her, to no avail. The both of them took her back out to the post and whipped her until she passed out. She awakened to a burning sensation across her back as it was pressed over and over again into the hard dirt and more pain between her legs as David pulled his trousers on and Isaiah rose and fell on top of her. She was in far too much pain to fight them off the second time.

As a result, she was having a baby. Sally never cried out while they were hurting her, and she did not cry out as the contractions grew stronger and stronger. She continued to swing the scythe well after the rush of warmth ran down her legs and the greedy soil beneath her feet consumed her life bearing fluids. Harsh grunts escaped her throat, even as she tried to hold them back. The woman nearest her almost missed catching Sally as her body failed and she swooned, clutching her tightened belly as she fell to the moist ground.

———

Cecilia Smith stomped into the room. "I done told y'all to go to bed and quit all that noise! I'm gonna call that ghost lady to come get y'all."

Their Mommy was angry. She was always angry.

"Don't call the ghost lady, Mommy. I tried to change Savvy's dipey but I made a mess. I'm sorry, Mommy." Tariq stood over his baby sister where she lay playing with her dirty diaper on the floor, grasping the contents clumsily in her hands and moving towards her mouth. Tariq brushed at her hands until she dropped the refuse back onto the floor. He didn't want to leave his spot over her in case Mommy decided to spank him. She often hit both of them so they would cry and fall asleep.

Cecilia grabbed his chubby arm and pinched him so hard he cried out. "I'm calling old spooky Sally now. Sally! Come get these bad ass kids!"

———

Sally pushed the way Tati Jane told her to, gripping the sweaty bedclothes in her aching fists. Nothing had ever hurt the way trying to birth the baby did. She tried to focus on doing what she was told but she wanted instead to escape from her tortured body and leave the husk to wither in the pain that threatened to destroy it.

Finally, feeling something inside her burst free, the baby fell out into Jane's competent hands, waiting at Sally's feet. The older woman rubbed the baby with an old cloth and his indignant screams echoed through the dank cabin. The pain became a distant memory and another feeling replaced it inside Sally. She raised up slightly to see what the baby looked like. Now that he was no longer housed inside her body, she started to think of him as a separate being from her, one she longed to get to know.

"Boy. Big strong, strapping boy." Jane wrapped the baby in another cloth and pressed him into the space Sally's arm made as she half reclined on the cot. Jane eased her down, back into her delivery position, so she could finish her work. As she pressed on Sally's still swollen abdomen, the girl watched the baby in awe. She took in his tiny face and head, still shaped like a cone where he had passed from her body. She weakly unwrapped the cloth to examine his hands. She wanted to see his feet and his legs, but she was afraid to completely unwrap him.

Sally loved the baby, despite the circumstances that had brought him to her. She went back out to the field after two days of bed rest, afforded the additional time only because Jane had to stitch her up after the birth. It hurt for her to walk, but David had come into the cabin yelling that she had to get back to her duties. Jane showed her how to make a sling for the baby so she could carry him outside with her and allow him to feed while she worked.

The miracle of birth had given her ample milk to feed her son and he grew fat in the first month. She talked to him and told him the stories she had heard around the plantation, tales of freedom and royal ancestors. Sally was a quick learner and she took to caring for the baby easily. She still marveled in his perfection and often spent long hours in the night looking at him, dreaming of his freedom one day as she drifted off to sleep.

On one such night, the master came into the cabin she shared with other slave women and told the others to get out. Sally tried to free herself from the bondage of slumber to comprehend what was happening. The man wrenched her baby from her arms and handed him off to David, who had followed him inside.

"Time to get that one off to the Pendersons." The baby started to wail and Sally's breasts tingled in response, milk blooming on the front of her dress. Master eyed the growing spots and fumbled with his belt. He pushed Sally back down onto her cot and raped her as she cried out for her baby. The sticky milk running from her breasts covered the front of his shirt. She could not stop him from defiling her.

Sally closed her eyes and found she could almost allow herself to escape her body to go and try to find her son, to see where they were taking him. She had never heard of the Pendersons and she did not know the whereabouts of their plantation. She did not know where to look. Knowing she would likely never see him again hurt her soul much more than her master had hurt her body.

———

"Mommy! No. I'm sorry. I'm sorry. Her dipey was hurting her."

She glanced at Savannah and bent to take a look at the baby's bottom through the unsecured side of her diaper Tariq hadn't been able to close. She sucked her teeth and went to the rickety chest of drawers in front of the lone window in the room and rummaged around the top. The tube of diaper ointment she grasped was flattened, but she squeezed it, anyway, putting the tiny drop of cream on her daughter's buttocks and fastened the diaper.

"We hungry." Tariq sniffled and held his arm where she had pinched him. He backed away from Cecilia when she turned her gaze to him. Her face had softened slightly and she returned to the chest of drawers. She brushed small roaches off the open packet of crackers and handed them to Tariq.

"Share with your sister. Y'all eat these and go to sleep." Cecilia located two bottles with murky liquid inside. She sprinkled a sample onto her hand and tasted it. "And take these."

Tariq had already tried to get Savannah to drink the warm, leftover lemonade in her bottle, but she had thrown it across the room and whined. He agreed with her that it was nasty. But he didn't tell Mommy that. He sat down and broke a hard cracker into two pieces and handed one to his little sister.

Satisfied, Cecilia closed the door. This time, she locked it behind her.

———

Sally had just turned eleven years old when she had the twins. Two beautiful baby girls with heads full of kinky curly hair. Tati Jane sucked her teeth as she worked to stop Sally's bleeding that time, muttering under her breath about devils and hellfire. The birth had been difficult on Sally's young body, but she felt all the struggle had been worth it when she held her daughters. She envisioned them growing up healthy, released from the bondage of slavery. Sally heard the slaves talking in their quarters and several openly discussed a day when they would be freed people. Freedom. To grow. To love. To see her babies grow up this time, into women who would go on to raise families of their own.

She sang to her daughters as they nestled deeply inside a special sling Tati Jane crafted just for Sally. She returned to the field after a week, due to the extensive damage her body sustained carrying and delivering two babies at her young age. Sally could not move as quickly as she had before their birth. She tried to keep up and stay out of the memory of master and Isiah and David. She did her work and kept her head down, not even engaging in conversation with her fellow enslaved people. She only wanted to sing to her babies and feed them, willing herself to live more fully in the imagined world she desired for their future.

Sally and her daughters did not remain invisible for long. David came to her in the field one day when the babies were a few weeks old and snatched them from their mother's breasts. Sally howled and beat helplessly at him as he headed toward the big house carrying her most precious cargo. Isiah intercepted them and pulled out the whip he loved to carry. His vicious lashes burned across her face, her still leaking breasts, her abdomen. He struck her over and over again until she lay prone in the yard, a bloodied, heartbroken mass.

She never saw her daughters again.

The master and David and Isaiah continued to violate Sally relentlessly and she remained pregnant every year until she was twenty. Each time her births produced live babies the men took them away from her. Sally spent more and more time outside her body than inside where the pain of her childlessness seared her soul. After the last birth, Tati Jane pronounced Sally's womb exhausted and she could not bear any more children.

David decided she would then go to work in the big house since his wife had just had their son and Sally could help feed him and take care of their toddler while his wife convalesced. He also figured it would be easier to get to Sally when he wanted her to perform other duties if she were already inside the house and not out in the cabins.

Wordlessly, Sally acquiesced and followed him to her new charges. She listlessly picked the infant up in her arms and held her to her breast when the baby cried. Her milk production, meant solely for her own babies, did not respond to the baby and soon there were only trickles coming down. She spent long days chasing the toddler with the infant hanging from her breast because their mother did not want to spend any time with them.

Then came the night Sally escaped her mortal coil for the length of the entire night. She was no longer tethered to her tortured life of bondage. She knew true freedom for the first time in her life. When Sally awakened the next morning, she felt excitement for the first time in years. She had not felt anything since her last baby was stolen—they took the last of her life from her with him. Now she was renewed, ready for a new life. With all her babies.

Kneeling in front of the cot where the toddler slept, she held a feather pillow over his head until his small body stopped fighting. She picked the infant up and held her tightly against her bosom, covering her little face until she, too, became still. She pressed kisses onto their sweet little faces and then walked down the stairs and into the yard underneath the hanging tree.

"What have you done, you Black bitch?" David's hoarse cries woke the entire plantation. Isaiah followed quickly behind him with his trusty whip. Sally could hear David's wife wailing from inside the house, but she sounded far away. David kicked her until she fell down. Sally hummed and Isaiah cracked his whip on the other side of her body.

"Get a rope!" Isaiah yelled to one of the enslaved house boys and the child ran to do as he was told.

Master joined the melee and barked additional orders. "You are going straight to hell! I damn you for all eternity!"

Sally forced a laugh from between her swollen lips. "I have been in hell. Now I will be redeemed. I will find my babies and we will be free."

The three men wrapped the retrieved rope around her neck and dragged her to the big tree in the yard. David continued to pummel her with blows until his father moved him so they could complete Sally's punishment.

She had left her body long before Master pronounced her death. David, Isaiah, and the enslaved people gathered in the yard locked their astonished gazes on a figure retreating from where they stood. Sally walked away from them, holding David's daughter in one arm and she held the hand of a small boy with her other. David's son and two other children walked solemnly behind Sally's apparition, as her body hung from the tree, swaying in time to her mournful lullaby carried by the wind, drifting away with her and her children.

———

Tariq heard a sweet song coming from somewhere outside the bedroom window. He went to see where it was coming from. Mommy always told them to stay out the windows, but he had to see. It wasn't Mommy. She never sang to them. A nice lady was calling him and Savannah. He stood on his tiptoes and he could see her clearly, where she stood under the streetlight, waving to him.

"My babies. Come with me so we can be together forever."

She was so pretty. For the first time in a week, Tariq wasn't hungry anymore. And he was warm. He gently shook Savannah awake and took her to the window with him. His baby sister cooed and babbled to the pretty lady. She had other kids with her and they all rose high in the night sky until they were right outside the eighth-floor window, smiling at Tariq and Savannah.

"My beautiful babies. Come." She stretched out her hand and Tariq helped Savannah up onto the window ledge and into the woman's arms. He followed, warmed by her embrace. Happy to be with other children. She would take care of them.

"Now we must go get my other babies."

Cecilia Smith stepped into the room just in time to watch her two children disappear into the arms of the woman floating in the window.

RECKLESS

RAYNE KING

"How long are we staying for?" Otto asks.

"Not long," Wesley says.

Otto looks at his friend and recognizes the familiar smirk, knowing it signals reckless behavior ahead. This same night has already played out countless times throughout the course of their friendship: Wesley making a promise he has no real plans on keeping, while Otto pretends to believe him. Parties give Wesley a reason to drink excessively. Drinking alone makes you an alcoholic; drinking at parties makes you social. Or at least that's what Wesley tells himself as he parks his coupe, an American beater from the early nineties that runs on fumes and bad intentions. Otto, on the other hand, instantly regrets agreeing to tag along when he sees the surrounding cars and people trickling into the house. But he has come out of support for his friend, understanding Wesley is having immense trouble coping with a recently broken heart.

Wesley would never admit to the pain he's feeling; he wears a mask of indifference, but Otto has known him for too long to be fooled into thinking he doesn't hurt.

Wesley exits the car first and waits for Otto to climb out before speaking: "Please don't be weird," he says.

Otto looks at him from across the roof of the car. "Why would you say that?" he asks, the sun dipping behind the mountains in the distance, the fading light hitting him in a way that makes it look like he's catching fire.

"I know how you get, that's all." "Yeah, well, I know how *you* get too." "What is that supposed to mean?" Otto scoffs. "Okay, Wes, play dumb."

———

The party begins slowly.

People drink beer or fix themselves simple cocktails. A game of beer pong gets going and some of the partygoers crowd the table, waiting for their turns to play. Out on the patio, a small group passes around a blunt, getting high. Music plays softly, coming from speakers stationed around the house. The quiet atmosphere grants Otto a degree of comfortability he is unused to in social settings. Parties have always put him on edge, riddling him with anxiety. Complete opposite of Wesley, who seems to only ever be truly alive when attending one. It was a characteristic that caused Otto to pity his friend - the idea of never being content with your own company was deeply saddening. He also knows how reckless Wesley is capable of becoming when he drinks. But so far everything is fine. Wesley behaves himself, sticking to beer. He doesn't touch any of the liquor bottles lined up along the countertop.

Yet, anyway.

Otto sneaks into the kitchen and helps himself to a beer from the fridge. Thinking he has some time before Wesley turns careless, Otto wanders into the living room and settles into the corner. He sips his beer while absently watching a television show that - he guesses - was turned on for background noise.

The night creeps on.

Newcomers arrive steadily, and the house begins to liven up. As the mood of the party shifts, so does Otto's. No longer does he feel at ease; on the contrary, he's nervous and concentrates on the show, hoping the mindless program manages to retain his attention enough to keep him distracted from the surging crowd. His sanctuary is dismantled when a group of rowdy partygoers infiltrates his immediate area, taking up the seats around him.

Otto gives idle chit-chat an honest try before the knots in his stomach become too much to bear and he worries that he is on the verge of a panic attack. He excuses himself from the conversation unfolding, deciding to locate Wesley in hopes of convincing him to leave early. He threads his way through the packed house, unaware that he grips the neck of his beer bottle so tightly the whites in his knuckles show.

Otto's search for Wesley proves unsuccessful.

The music is blaring now and the house shakes from people dancing.

His heart beats against his chest, like a frenzied bird trying to break out of its cage. The walls close in on him and his vision blurs.

He overhears that someone is handing out Valiums and seeks out the source. He seemingly blinks and finds himself holding a pill in the palm of his hand. He throws it back, washing it down with the rest of the beer. Slight relief, knowing he'll be able to calm down once the pill kicks in.

Soon, he begins to float.

He shoulders through bodies until he arrives at the door leading to the backyard. He slides the glass door open and shuffles out onto the patio. The night air is cool and refreshing in contrast to the stuffy interior of the house. He inhales deeply, smelling the sweet aroma of the woods bordering the property. The mounting sense of claustrophobia dissipates as he scans the vast estate. Looking at the mountains, he feels insignificant, and the knowledge provides a surprising amount of relief, understanding his existence is trivial and the intense stress he experiences is ultimately meaningless compared to the world at large.

A handful of people occupy the backyard, piling wood into a fire pit. Someone douses the logs with lighter fluid, steps back, sparks a match, and tosses the matchstick into the pit. The fire catches instantly and the flames grow high, rippling from the autumn breeze coming down from the neighboring mountains. The fire reveals the faces circling the pit, and Otto sees his man.

Wesley is hammered, teetering on the edge of oblivion. "W-where have you been?" he stammers, holding a bottle of bourbon at his side.

"You said we weren't going to be here long," Otto says softly. "We haven't been," Wesley says, taking a swig from the bottle. "...can we please leave, Wes?"

"I'm not ready to leave yet."

"You know this part of the reason why she left you, right?"

Wesley's eyes glisten and reflect the licking flames. "I don't know what you're talking about."

"Come on, man."

Wesley's demeanor hardens. "Have a drink with me," he says, redirecting the conversation."

"I don't want to."

Wesley steps beside Otto, draping his arm around him. Holding the bottle up for Otto's inspection, he sloshes the amber liquid around by flicking his wrist. "Don't make me drink alone."

"I thought that's what the party is for."

"It's an excuse; everybody here might as well be a stranger." Otto sighs. "You're okay to still drive, right?"

"Of course I am."

———

They finish off the bourbon together.

Wesley throws the empty bottle into the pit, watching as the glass darkens from the heat.

The friends sit next to each other on large wooden lawn chairs. Nobody else remains outside, only the two of them.

"Why're you like this?" Otto says, his words slurring.

Wesley looks at him, blinking slowly. "Like what?"

"You can never just drink for a good time."

"What're you talking about? I'm having a good time right now."

The booze has loosened Otto's tongue, and he speaks in earnest: "No, it's like you always drink to prove a point."

"Maybe I am, then."

"But what is it? What's the point you're trying to make?"

"It's like this, I guess…drinking lets me forget about who I am. At least for a little while, I can pretend to be someone else."

"What's wrong with who you are sober?"

Wesley smiles, but the expression is forced and masks a deep sadness below the surface. "I don't know, maybe I just don't like him."

A clear sky reveals a starry canvas above. Wesley holds his fingers in the shape of a gun and aims at a star. He pulls the imaginary trigger. "Bang," he says.

"Why'd you do that?" Otto asks.

Wesley shrugs. "Make a wish."

"That only counts if the star is falling."

"Then don't," Wesley says, getting out of his chair. "Let's go back inside."

"I'm not feeling up for that."

"Okay, stay here." Wesley stands around for a moment. "We'll leave soon," he says.

Otto looks up at him. "Really?"

"Yeah," he says, walking back toward the house. The star Wesley aimed at drops from the sky.

Otto notices this and turns around, calling after Wesley so he can see it too, but he has already stumbled back indoors.

———

The bourbon has turned Wesley melancholic and his mind keeps returning to the hole she left behind in his chest. He continues to drink like he holds a grudge against his liver, attempting to drink himself into a stupor so he can stop thinking about her. At least for one night.

He becomes aggressive the more he drinks, looking to pick a fight. If he can't make himself blackout from drinking, then he'll provoke someone into doing it for him. He bumps into a pair of guys on purpose without apologizing. They let it slide, but Wesley makes a nasty comment. He is told to calm down, but responds by flinging insults at them. Tensions rise.

Wesley shoves one of them, and a brawl breaks out. Two against one, Wesley doesn't stand a chance. But he's okay with that. He manages to hold his own for a little bit, tussling.

Then they stop playing around and cease to pull their punches.

One drives a fist into his stomach hard enough to knock the wind out of him. The other lands a haymaker, busting his face open.

They pummel him until he's on the floor in the fetal position. Finally they stop, breathing heavy from their efforts.

He uncurls and sprawls out on the floor, laughing through bloody teeth. They call him fucking crazy.

She used to say the same about him.

They yank him to his feet and drag him out of the house.

He protests, trying to pull himself free, but really he knows this is what he wanted all along. Something to distract him.

Otto overhears the commotion coming from the front of the house and jogs around to investigate. His gut tells him that Wesley is responsible for the uproar, and as he rounds the corner he sees Wesley illuminated by the floodlights, tossing up both middle fingers in the direction of the house. As Otto gets closer, he sees Wesley's face is smashed; pity and worry overcome him.

"What happened to you?"

Wesley turns to face Otto. He runs his tongue across his split upper lip, wincing against the copper taste. "Fuck them," he says.

"You always do this."

"Fuck you too," Wesley says, stumbling off into the darkness to find his car.

Otto goes after him, catching up in no time. "What's wrong with you?"

"Are you coming?"

"Where?"

"I'm leaving."

"You can't leave like this."

"Fine stay here, I don't care."

Between getting in the car with Wesley or staying behind at a party he doesn't want any part of, Otto puts his faith in his longtime friend and climbs into the passenger seat.

Wesley fires the engine up.

He peels out of the driveway, reversing hard, spitting up gravel. He slams the shifter into first gear, punches the gas; the tires spin briefly before catching traction. Racing away from the house, the lights dim into the backdrop and soon they are cruising along the lonely country roads.

Wesley is speeding, the needle climbing steadily upwards. He takes a turn too wide and feels the car tilt. He's too drunk to care and laughs at the close call. Otto, however, grabs the handle above his head and braces a hand against the dashboard. "Slow down," he says.

"Relax."

"Acting like this only justifies her leaving you; it's not going to make you feel better." Wesley doesn't want to listen to reasoning; he wishes to take his car into the void.

Trees lining the road rush by in a blur.

Another sharp turn, Wesley teases the brake, hugging the shoulder tightly this time around. Otto breathes a little easier in response, thinking Wesley is winding down.

He's wrong.

Once the turn is cleared and the road straightens out, Wesley pushes the clutch in and shifts into a higher gear. The RPM meter drops off as the torque is released, but then it begins to build again as Wesley drives the gas pedal into the floor.

Tragedy strikes.

Wesley sees double, two roads ahead.

In a panic he cuts the wheel too fast, trying to get back onto whichever one he thinks is concrete. The motion is too sudden for the car to withstand and it swerves into the opposing lane. Wesley tries to regain control by jerking the wheel violently clockwise. He overcorrects and loses complete control as the car begins to spin. He wrestles with the steering wheel desperately; Otto screams, seeing they are on a collision course with a telephone pole. Wesley knows this too, and at the last second cuts the wheel further in hopes of directing the car away from the pole.

This last change in direction causes the wheels to lift off the ground and the car begins to roll.

Wesley shuts his eyes tightly and prepares to die. Otto is robbed of even that.

When the car rolls, the passenger side window shatters, sending shards of glass into the side of Otto's face. Another devastating rotation crushes the door, pinning him to his doom. The car finally collides with the pole and Otto is crushed upon impact, his mangled body hanging upside down as the car stabilizes.

The airbag knocked Wesley out for a moment.

He regains consciousness quickly and realizes in a vague sense that he is seeing the world upended. He unbuckles himself, saying Otto's name, as he drops to the roof of the car.

He crawls out of the wreck.

The smell of smoke and leaking coolant is pungent, and in his frenzied state, Wesley fears the car will explode similar to a movie. That is not the case; he sways as he lifts himself from the metal carnage, dizzy. Steam rises from the wreckage, the hot radiator fluid pouring from the busted engine. The side he escaped from appears somewhat salvageable. The passenger side, though, is entirely destroyed, crushed beyond recognition against the telephone pole.

Realizing the horror, Wesley crawls back inside the car, yelling for Otto to wake up.

Wake up.

Wake up.

His brain won't let him process the carnage his eyes relay to it - as a protective measure, it feeds the information to him slowly. He attempts to tug Otto out of the car, yanking him as he shimmies backward. The effort is futile. Otto has become intertwined with the heap of metal.

Barely comprehending what has happened, Wesley vaguely accepts that he won't be able to dislodge his friend from the wreckage.

Outside of the car again, he sits back and grabs his head in disbelief. He sobs uncontrollably, beginning to realize what he has done.

Suddenly, he feels eyes on him.

He looks up in hopes of seeing someone who can help the hopeless situation.

The headlights are shattered, but the taillights remain intact, and the red glow reveals a figure standing across the road, watching him.

Wesley shoots up, standing. "Help! Please!"

The watcher doesn't answer his cry for help, only continues to look seemingly without emotion, as if observing him.

"We need help!" Wesley yells, stumbling across the road toward the watcher.

As he gets closer, the watcher evaporates, almost whoever it was hadn't been there at all. Wesley sniffles, wipes away the tears and snot running down his face.

Again, the same sensation of being watched hits him.

He looks up the mountainside and sees the watcher standing among the trees, looking downward at him.

"What're you doing? We need fucking help!" The watcher stays motionless.

Wesley runs uphill in pursuit, spurred on by confusion and

outrage. The watcher doesn't move, allowing Wesley to come close.

Wesley looks at the watcher and immediately regrets it.

An abstract, featureless face stares back at him, burrowing into his soul. He staggers backward and loses his footing, falling down the hill.

Surviving the tumble, Wesley is fast to look back at where the watcher had been standing, but nothing is there now, only the skeletons of leafless trees.

He thinks he's losing his mind over killing his friend. Maybe he's correct.

Or maybe not.

As he turns his back, the same intense feeling of being watched hits him.

He tries to ignore it, beginning to trot down the road in hopes of seeing a car or finding a house. His footsteps are wobbly and he has difficulty staying upright. He stumbles and manages to save himself from tripping by leaning against a tree trunk for support.

Watchful eyes on him again.

He looks up and sees the mysterious watcher squatting on a large branch above, staring down at him.

Wesley screams and takes off running.

The watcher follows him the entire time, popping up everywhere, judging.

After being tormented by the watcher stalking him, Wesley is fortunate enough to discover a long driveway. He hustles up it, feeling his way through the darkness. All he finds at the end of the driveway is an abandoned barn. The bright moon silhouettes the watcher, standing on top of the barn, staring intently at Wesley.

Wesley halts movement and drops to his knees, crying. Heartbroken and horrified.

"Otto," he whispers. "I'm sorry."

PERCHTA

BRENNAN LAFARO

The slam of a car door carries through the cracked window of Seth Weber's upstairs bedroom, sending a shiver racing up his spine. His father is home. The front door squeaks gently as if trying to disguise the mood of the man behind it. Then silence. Too much of it for comfort. Seth can't decide whether that means his father is searching for a reason to yell at him or an excuse to bypass his room completely. Ever since the accident, the stairs often bother Henry Weber's knee too much to make the trip.

The evening drags on and Seth almost believes himself safe. Then the first footstep thumps against the bottom stair. Seconds stretch out between each successive thud. Every beat of silence makes his heart pound faster. There must be a direct connection between how slowly each strenuous footfall takes and how much patience will remain in his father when he reaches the top of the stairs.

Finally, the lumbering thumps stop in front of Seth's door, and it swings open gently. Not locked, never locked. Not in this house. Frigid winter air pours in through the open window. Despite the cold, a line of sweat trickles down Seth's temple.

Compared to the polite creak of the front door, the hinges on Seth's door squeal a desperate warning.

Disheveled hair and bloodshot eyes appear in the frame, telling Seth all he needs to know. Henry Weber leaves every weekday morning at eight a.m. sharp and returns just after six, but Seth wonders, not for the first time, if he actually still goes to work or just sleeps the day away in his car. Seth swallows the guilt that piggybacks on the thought.

Food, water, and shelter, he thinks. The three things everyone needs to survive according to some guy named Maslow who clearly never shared a house with someone who didn't give a shit whether he lived or died.

Harsh, yes, but as Henry stares through his son, Seth knows it's true.

"Goin' to bed?" Henry slurs as he shuffles into the room. If the muddy words didn't give him away, the stench would've. Seth recognizes the pungent odor of whiskey better than any fifth grader should. He also understands short answers as the most effective tool to move this obligatory interaction along without having it go south.

"Yes, sir."

His father responds with a quick nod as his eyes wander the room. Henry never served in any branch of the armed forces, but Seth habitually calls him sir. It makes him more amenable, usually helping to get him on his way more quickly.

Tonight, unfortunately, the strategy bears no fruit.

Henry parks himself on the end of Seth's bed, peering thoughtfully at the calendar. Every box displays a broad red X, as though Seth has dug in deep enough with the marker to draw blood.

"Son of a bitch," Henry whispers. "Been two years tonight."

Screams. Crunching metal.

Seth's gaze betrays him, flitting toward a framed picture on his bedside table. A woman. Her long brown curls and turtleneck make her look like a remnant of a bygone era and her bold white smile radiates a warmth that watches over Seth every night.

Henry clears his throat. "Get a chance to eat?"

"Yes, sir. There was a can of soup left." Seth lowers his eyes from the photo and locks them on the tattered beige carpet.

"Don't suppose you left any for me."

"No, sir. Sorry, sir."

Henry exhales louder than necessary. He raises a hand to run through his hair, pausing as Seth flinches. "No, 'course not. You don't give a shit. Not like you're the one's got to go to the grocery store or figure out a way to pay for the trip. You've done nothing but sit on your dead ass since the school sent you home. Christ. When you go back, anyway?"

"Two days," says Seth, willing his voice not to shake.

"Two days, *sir*."

"Two days, sir."

"That's better."

Seth's eyes dart to the photograph and this time his father catches it. Henry bites his lip and scowls, then reaches out and slams the picture face down. The muffled crunch of glass seems to echo through the tiny bedroom and Seth's heart sinks down near his toes.

Shards of glass. A metallic scent.

The scar that runs along Seth's arm throbs.

When Henry speaks again, his voice is flat and devoid of emotion. "Shit, kid. You know it hurts me to see that. Not like she's comin' back."

And it's your fault, Seth wants to scream. He bites his tongue so hard he tastes blood.

Henry returns his stare to the calendar. A grin creeps onto his face and Seth's stomach drops down next to his heart. "She ever tell you about the Perchta?"

Mom. His father can't even say her name.

Seth shakes his head, furrowing his brow at the strange word.

"Her mama used to tell her the story when she was little. Goddamn devil woman, you ask me."

Seth nods because Henry expects it. His grandmother is the furthest thing from the devil, but Henry hasn't allowed her to visit over the last two years. Not for her lack of trying, either. Often, Seth has spotted his grandmother watching the house, standing on the sidewalk as if waiting for an invitation. Henry would call the police, but Grandmother always vanished before they arrived.

"Apparently the old woman used to hear the stories in the old country," says Henry. "Swears she even saw it once. They had Santa, same as the kids here, but a week later—on New Year's Eve—the Perchta would come on down from the mountains once all the kids were asleep." Smirking, he walks his fingers down the scar on Seth's forearm. The hair stands at attention and Seth yanks his arm away. Henry's smile disappears.

"Now if I remember right, the kids that were good, hardworking and respected their parents, they got rewarded. More gifts. Almost like a second Christmas. The other ones? The lazy, greedy little bastards who caused problems? Can't shut the fuck up for two seconds and cause accidents? What do you think happened to them?"

Seth's throat goes dry and his face grows hot. "They didn't get anything," he mumbles.

"Oh no, that's where the Perchta is different from the jolly fuckin' fat man. The bad kids don't just get a lump of coal. The Perchta takes a razor-sharp talon and guts 'em like a turkey. The next morning, their parents find them in bed, little faces frozen in horror. Instead of hearts, lungs, and all the other stuff that makes your body tick, the Perchta stuffs them full of straw, full of rocks, garbage. Pretty much anything she can find lying around."

Seth imagines what his face must look like. Pale and frozen like the children in the story. "Is... Is it a witch?"

"Yeah, I suppose that's as good a way to put it as any."

Seth wants his father to leave. More than anything, he wants him to leave, but he can't help himself. "What does she look like?"

Henry shifts closer to Seth. "That's my favorite part. It depends whether you've been good, or a disrespectful little shit. The kids who get rewarded, they see a young woman, draped in white and surrounded by pure light. Supposed to be beautiful. Radiant, even."

"What about the other kids?"

"A withered old hag, and she's not alone. You know you're in deep shit if the Straggele show up."

He holds up a hand, anticipating Seth's next question. "These *things*, monsters really, they're about the size of a kid, maybe a bit shorter than you. They're covered head to toe in shaggy, brown hair. I saw a drawing once, and I'll never forget it. They got this patch of skin around their blank white eyes. Kinda looks like a mask, with sharp red horns poking out, sticking up above their heads. Not something you want to run into after midnight."

Henry's grin spreads from ear to ear. "The Perchta is the one who stuffs the lazy children, but it's the Straggele who tear out everything vital in the first place. Now, I ain't ever seen one, but what do you think they do with all them organs once they get 'em out?"

Seth can't move. Can't breathe.

Henry stands up. "I think that's probably enough. Leave the rest to your imagination."

He walks to the door. "I've got some shit needs doing tomorrow around the house, and I'm countin' on your help. Least you can do, I guess. Wouldn't want to be branded a lazy kid, would you?"

Henry flicks the lights off and limps out of the room, closing the door behind him.

———

"Quit your damn squealin'"

The words echo through Seth's head as he slides across the backseat of the car. Oncoming headlights stream in through the windshield. All he'd wanted was a bathroom stop, and instead, the car careens out of control while he dodges his father's swatting hands.

His mother reaches back from the passenger seat a split second before the headlights steal his vision, only for a moment, and then the crunch of metal closes in on him. It's the loudest sound he can recall in his short life. Her outstretched hand vanishes in a swirl of chaos. Seth tries to cover his ears, but he is suddenly floating. The seatbelt tries to hold him in place while pebbles of glass slice and sting his bare skin. A jagged metal dagger blazes up his forearm and warm wetness dribbles down to his fingers.

From the front seat, a high scream pierces the symphony of screeching metal. Seth almost forgets that he's airborne until gravity slams the sedan's ruined skeleton to the asphalt. The car grinds to a halt, sending sparks into the air like dandelion seeds. His father's face smacks into the seat with a sound like a plate dropped onto a dinner table. The sharp tang of whiskey mixes with something unfamiliar, almost metallic.

Quit your damn squealin'.

The screams continue, but sound far away, muddled as if underwater, then everything goes blurry and quiet. Darkness creeps in from the edges of his vision.

The gloom of night gives way to an impossibly bright light, white as angel's robes. The first face he sees assures him that he hasn't died and gone to heaven. Wrinkles line his grandmother's eyes. Rather than making her look old and tired, they contain echoes of concern. When Seth opens his eyes, the wrinkles don't recede, but reflect the creases at the corners of a forming smile.

"I've got you," she says.

"Mom," Seth mumbles and Grandmother's face can no longer support her smile.

A small shake of her head and tears gather in her eyes. "But I will always protect you."

The room swirls, a white haze clawing at his eyes. His grandmother's face dissolves. Somewhere in the distance machines beep and murmured conversations distort.

He doesn't remember what happens next.

———

Seth sits straight up in his soaking wet bed, afraid at first that he had wet the sheets. No, only sweat. The car accident. The image of his grandmother's face dances in front of his eyes like a sunspot.

His eyes adjust to the darkness and as his grandmother's face fades to memory, her story comes into sharp relief.

Perchta.

The settling creaks of the house make him think of furry brown creatures pacing the hall. Each time the moonlight glints in through his window, he braces for it to reveal an ugly old woman, ready to plunge a glistening, pointed talon into his stomach.

The phantom pressure of the imaginary Perchta's claw transforms into a pressing need to use the bathroom. After a few moments, he can't ignore his bursting bladder any longer. He sucks in a breath and lets his legs slide out from under the covers one at a time. When his feet hit the floor and nothing snarls from the shadows, he exhales. Keeping his eyes shut to a slit, he dashes to the light switch and flips it on. One at a time, he opens his eyes. No Straggele. Not in this room, anyway.

The bathroom is two doors away, but the hallway seems to have grown miles in either direction once the sun went down. Seth shuts his eyes tight and runs for it, dragging one hand along the wall to feel for the knob. He yanks it open and throws himself inside, shutting the door louder than he means to. Blood pounds in his ears and he pants inside the small bathroom. The whirring of the fan drones overhead. Seth's pulse quickens, due in equal parts to the inevitable arrival of the Perchta and the chance he might have woken his father with that slammed door. Henry Weber does not tolerate slammed doors.

Seth checks the lock and turns toward the toilet. Whatever peril might lie outside the door, nature won't wait for it. He never imagined the sound of urine splashing into the toilet bowl would be comforting, but it drowns out the house's ambient noise. When he finishes, he flushes the toilet and listens.

What is that shuffling sound? The clicking of ragged toenails tapping the thin carpet?

There one moment and then lost beneath the hum of the fan.

A groan.

An unhappy floorboard or the growl of a small creature?

Seth looks at the bathtub. For a moment, he thinks of sleeping there.

Another groan. Definitely something in the hall. Waiting for him to come out.

Seth holds as still as possible, not daring to breathe, willing whatever it is to go away.

He waits for the sound to repeat. Another glance at the bathtub. Then he shakes his head. What would his father think if he woke at the crack of dawn to find Seth in the locked bathroom, asleep in the filthy tub? He shudders to think of the consequences.

Thirty seconds pass without further clamor, and Seth opens the door to a crack. As he peers out, he catches the vanishing silhouette of a figure descending the stairs and his heart rockets up into his throat. A halo of white light seems to float over its shoulders.

He eases the door shut again, as quietly as he can.

"The Perchta," he whispers. The hair on the back of his neck stands up straight as his mind runs in circles. Fear turns to anger as he realizes what's happened.

"This is exactly what he wanted," Seth whispers to himself. "To make me upset. He probably saw me open the door and now he's downstairs laughing, knowing he has me scared half to death." The more Seth thinks about it, the more sense it makes, the angrier he gets. He knows he might regret it, but for the time being, he doesn't care.

He throws open the door, spilling the light from the bathroom into the hallway and down the stairs. No trace of the figure, and certainly no Straggele. Creeping down the stairs, he listens for any unusual sounds. No footsteps, no television. Suddenly an odd grumbling perks his ears up, similar to a running vacuum cleaner.

A bestial smell stops Seth at the base of the stairs. It reminds him of the donkeys at the local zoo.

The strange murmur cuts off abruptly as he enters the living room. His father sits on the couch, watching the muted television. It's black and white static casts strange patterns across the walls like writhing ghosts. Seth tiptoes toward the television, as softly as possible, expecting his father's head to spin around at any moment. Instead, his father stares straight ahead.

As he rounds the couch, Seth understands why Henry hasn't noticed his arrival. The soup roils in Seth's stomach, threatening to erupt all over the carpet at what has become of Henry Weber. The man's glassy eyes reflect the black and white flickering of the television, remaining fixed on the screen even in death. They are open impossibly wide, as though in his last moment he believed seeing a bit more might help him understand what was happening to him. His mouth stretches in a silent scream, but it is Henry's chest that demands the most attention.

Something has ripped open Henry Weber's torso from throat to groin. Blood-soaked bits of straw poke out of the gaping cavity like earthworms seeking sunshine after rain. Rather than run, Seth steps closer.

"Rocks," he mumbles, feeling the blood drain from his face. "Rocks and trash."

And liquor bottles, he thinks.

Pebbles of glass sparkle from inside the ruined body of his father. Some come from the shattered whiskey containers, but others display a bluish tint like a car windshield.

A flash of light fills the living room, tearing Seth's attention from his father's body. He whips around, coming face-to-face with a beautiful woman wearing a white dress. The ethereal glow surrounding her removes any sliver of doubt regarding her identity.

"Grandma?" he asks.

The woman smiles, nearly as brilliant as the reassuring luminescence emanating from her.

The brightness recedes, throwing the wrinkles around her eyes into sharp relief.

Behind her are the Straggele. Four stocky outlines sheltering from the light. The hairy beasts appear docile and lethargic, like a pride of lions after a meal. The blood lining their mouths tells the story of what happens to the organs of the Perchta's victims; people who are callous and cruel.

That grumbling he heard from the stairs. It had been the Straggele eating.

Seth stares at the mythical creatures in his living room. The cyclone of conflicting emotions makes him dizzy.

"You killed him."

"I told you I would always protect you." Grandmother's voice resonates throughout the living room, radiating from the walls themselves.

Seth opens his mouth to reply, but nothing comes out.

"Those who are generous and hard-working are granted a reward. This is your reward, Seth." Her aura intensifies once more and Seth shields his eyes. When he can open them again, the Straggele are gone and the light with them.

Before him stands his grandmother, a slight woman with her hands folded in front of her. Any trace of magic has disappeared from her. She tilts her head in a questioning manner, waiting for Seth to speak.

"What are you?" He lowers his eyes, wincing at the rudeness in his question.

"I think you know," she answers softly. "I've waited years for the word to be spoken aloud in this house. To call me. And on this of all nights."

"Perchta."

The hint of a grimace crosses her face like a shadow. Then it's gone. She flicks her eyes toward Henry's body.

"If you needed to mourn, I would understand."

His tears refuse to fall. Shock, perhaps.

She nods and continues. "It was bad enough that *he* killed my daughter, my Angela. I could not allow him to do the same to you."

"Kill?"

"Or at least steal your life. It amounts to the same."

Seth sucks in a deep breath. The scent of blood, whiskey, and voided bowels mixes with the lingering aroma of Straggele stink and he feels his gorge rise again. "I can't stay here."

"No. On that, we agree." Grandmother holds out her hand. Flecks of blood spot her outstretched fingers like a trail of breadcrumbs leading to her feral claws. "Like I said, I will always protect you."

Seth hesitates for only a moment, then reaches out and clasps her hand. It burns cold, but only for a moment as swirling jets of blizzard white surround them, then carry them away.

LAUGH
AT US

TIM MEYER

ONE

It all started about a week after we moved into the new house, when I tripped over my own two feet. It wasn't until after—when I tried to get up—that I realized it wasn't my feet that caused the incident, it was my shoelaces. They'd been tied together.

I had fallen asleep on the couch while watching the baseball game (go Mets), and I guess after my third (or maybe fourth) beer of the afternoon, I couldn't keep my eyes open. I came back to life in the bottom of the ninth, just in time to watch the Mets' closer blow the save and lose the game—you know, in typical New York Mets September fashion. I was heading to the fridge to drown my sorrows with another pale ale but only got a step before taking that fateful tumble. I was able to brace myself for the fall, got my hands out in front, and prevented myself from falling flat on my face.

"Holy shit."

Bridgett rushed into the room at once, leaving behind the meal she was cooking in the kitchen. She had oven mitts on when she hustled to my side. "Baby, what happened?"

I glanced down at my feet, immediately knowing something wasn't quite right. The secured knot between my pair of Vans stared back at me, mocking me. Laughing at me. "I..." My first thought was to accuse Bridge, but in the ten years we'd known each other, six years of those a blissful marriage, not once had she ever pulled a prank on me. Okay, maybe *once*, maybe twice, but nothing like this, nothing that could have potentially injured me. I mean, I could have twisted an ankle, torn an ACL, or busted a tooth on the corner of the coffee table if I'd landed that way. No, Bridge wouldn't do this, but then again—she was the only other person in the house.

"What the..." she asked, looking at what I was looking at. "How did that happen?"

"Not sure," I said, scratching my scalp underneath my Mets cap. "I was going to ask you the same thing."

"What...you don't think I..."

"No, of course not. It's just..."

She looked around the room, shuddering like a cool chill blew in through an open window. But our windows were closed, and our doors were locked. Weren't they? It'd only been two weeks since we moved from the city to the sticks, and we were still getting used to country life. Probably didn't need to lock the doors and keep the windows shut, every entrance always secured, not when your closest neighbor's house can be covered up with a dime when looking on from your own porch, but still—it was hard for us to kick the city life's daily habits and routines.

"It's tied so well," I said, tugging at the laces, trying to loosen the knot. To free my feet, it took Bridge's nails working their way into the center of the entangled string and massaging the laces until they separated. After about a minute, I was able to spread my feet apart. "For a second I thought we were gonna have to cut them."

Bridge didn't seem amused. "You don't remember tying your shoelaces together?"

"No, why the hell would I do that?"

"It's just...weird."

I couldn't deny that. Weird it was, and I had no explanation. (And okay, secretly, I did think she'd done it. I just didn't want to accuse her. It felt wrong.)

"Maybe I did it in my sleep," I suggested, shrugging. "Did I ever tell you I used to sleepwalk when I was a kid?"

"I think so."

"I did all types of weird stuff. My parents caught me peeing in their closet one night."

"Gross."

"Indeed. Lost a lot of clothes in the yellow flood of '95."

"Chris, eww." She stood up, turned her back to me. "Dinner'll be ready in five minutes. Can I trust you won't hurt yourself between now and then?"

I showed her my empty palms. "No promises."

She rolled her eyes and disappeared into the kitchen. As she went, I stood on my now-free feet, swearing I smelled something that reminded me of smoked wood—and it wasn't coming from the kitchen where my wife was cooking dinner.

TWO

Later that night I awoke to sounds outside the bedroom window, a chirping that almost sounded like birds, but it was pitch black out and hours away from the usual morning birdsong. Couldn't have been birds. The noise stopped when I edged closer to the window, parted the blinds and peeked into the vast farmlands, of which Bridge and I were now owners. The silo next to the barn stood like an ancient pillar. Moonlight shone on its metal dome top. Then my eyes caught movement in the darkness. Subtle at first, but once my eyes adjusted, I saw it.

Not *it,* I guess—*them.*

Children. Or what I thought were children. Three of them sprinting from the barn, across the fields, and into the neighboring thicket that bordered the forest surrounding us. Laughing? They may have been laughing, that *might* have been what that sound was.

I couldn't go back to sleep that night. I lay in bed, staring up at the ceiling, listening to the silence and expecting to hear more of that strange chirping, or the laughter of delinquent children. I wish I could meet the parents of these brats. I mean, seriously? Who lets their kids roam the neighborhood at three in the morning?

My alarm went off at five, but I was already dressed, had my first coffee, and was ready to feed the animals.

Bridge slept in until seven, when she had to wake up for school.

"Sleep well?" she asked, coming up behind me as I dumped a tray full of slop into the pigs' trough. I turned around and didn't even answer her, just stared. She was beautiful. Not that she wasn't all the time, but she really outdid herself for the first day of class.

I tried to wipe the dumb smile off my face. "Not quite."

She taught high school English, and she'd been looking forward to a fresh start at a new school. For one, she'd have half the students. Secondly, she was hoping things would be more relaxed out here, away from the city. The administration at her old school was in shambles, and they—according to her—didn't know their asses from their elbows, and rarely did they have the teachers' backs when it came to discipline and dealing with unreasonable parents.

"I heard you up early," she said.

"Yeah, kept hearing things outside. There were kids—"

"Kids?" She looked concerned now. "What do you mean?"

"I heard something—a chirping or some animal sounds outside the window, at around three. I peeked out the window and saw a bunch of kids near the barn."

"Did you talk to them?"

"Talk to them? Hell no. I wasn't going out there."

She giggled. "Well, it was probably a couple of pranksters."

"Yeah, probably. Didn't notice any damage or anything to the barn, so they were probably just hanging out. Smoking reefer or something."

"Reefer?" She burst into more giggles. "I don't think they call it that anymore, old man."

I pushed back my graying strands from my eyes. "Have a great first day."

She kissed me and said goodbye, and then I went back to work.

An hour later, I saw it—what the kids had done in the barn.

And I almost screamed.

THREE

The vandalism was done with exterior paint, or at least that was my (and the officer that came out to look) best guess. The coating was still tacky.

"Children you say?" the cop asked, hands on his hips, not writing any of this down. I don't know the first thing about being a cop, but I expected him to take notes for the report I was filing.

"Three of them. At least I think it was three. It was dark. The moon was full, so I had—"

"They do anything else to the barn? Destroy or damage anything?" He looked around, inspecting the area for evidence.

"No, not that I saw. I looked thoroughly after I saw...well, that." *That* was a collection of weird symbols painted on one of the sidewalls, back near the horse stalls. They had used black paint, a generous application; the cryptograms dripped. I didn't notice the graffiti until I went to let the horses out to graze. At least a dozen symbols, none of them recognizable, all of them arranged in a circle, almost like numbers on a clock, only the circle was far from perfect. There were zig-zag patterns of lines in the center.

None of it made sense to me. And—given the look on the cop's face—none of it made sense to Officer Do-Nothing either.

"So, nothing was damaged and broken?" he asked.

"Well, no." I knew what he was getting at. "But, officer—with all due respect—I mean, I know it's just some paint, kids being kids and all of that, but this is going to take me hours to paint or strip. Time is money, y'know. Plus, I don't want them to keep coming back."

His mustache wiggled as he chewed over my counterpoint. "Well, I can write up a report if you want—"

"Yes, that's what I want."

He shot me a look like *thanks for creating extra work for me, jackass.* But I didn't care.

"Okay, fine. I'll do that. But just a word of advice. This ain't the city. Not much to do out here, so the kids get bored. Sometimes they get into a little harmless mischief. My advice? Have a laugh at it."

He said this with a smile, like it was a joke. Like I *should be* laughing at it.

I didn't even say another word to him. I walked him out of the barn and watched him leave in his cruiser.

Have a laugh, he said.

Ha. Yeah, right. Sure.

FOUR

"You can't obsess over this, Chris," Bridge said. She was already in bed, reading over her lesson plans for the following day. The new curriculum had her edgy. Who was being obsessive again?

"I'm not obsessing," I said, turning away from the window and moonlit glow outside. "I'm just...you know...observing things."

"You've been standing at the window for an hour now. It's almost midnight. Come to bed."

I did have to wake up early. So, I took one last look at the empty farm, then stood up, undressed, and climbed into bed, nuzzling up with my wife. She finally put her lesson plans on the nightstand.

"Just feel...invaded," I told her. "I mean, you have to admit— it's messed up. On a few different levels."

"It's just kids," she said. "At least they didn't break or destroy anything."

Maybe I was taking it too far. Guess I've always been that way, worrying about things that are smaller than they really are. It only took an hour to paint over the symbols. In the grand scheme of life, it was a minor inconvenience. Annoying, but since I already had the paint, it didn't cost me anything but time.

I went to bed feeling better about it.

But when I woke up and saw that someone had once again broken in and repainted the symbols on the same wall, the fire in my chest was reignited.

FIVE

The guy from the distribution company who came to pick up the bottled milk arrived around seven, when I was halfway done rolling out a fresh coat over the new symbols. He interrupted me with a catcall-like whistle.

I turned to him. "Oh hey, Dave."

"Someone conjuring up demons in here or what?" He just laughed.

Everyone seemed to think it was funny, and the funnier people thought it was, the more it pissed me off.

"No. Shit—maybe. Neighborhood kids keep breaking in and painting this weird shit on my walls. Fucking pranksters." I went on to tell him I was heading into town, finding the nearest Best Buy, and loading up on security equipment. I'd had enough.

"Kids, you say?"

I nodded. "Saw them two nights ago. They were running away from the barn, toward the woods."

"The woods? At night?"

"Three in the morning. It was full dark out."

"Hmm. That sound right to you?"

I hadn't thought about it at the time, but now that he mentioned it...why would they be running into the woods? At that hour? I didn't even see a flashlight. They were traveling in the moonlight with nothing else to light their way.

Not sure why, but my arms and neck broke out with gooseflesh.

"I mean," Dave said, pulling out his checklist and running through the inventory numbers for the pickup, "wouldn't kids be running toward the road at that hour."

"Maybe. I don't know. I didn't get a chance to ask them. Maybe I will when I catch the little shits in the act."

"I don't think it was kids," he said, almost sing-songlike.

My forehead bunched up, so much so it hurt. "What are you saying?"

He tucked the clipboard under his arm and had himself a look at the symbols. As he spoke, he pointed at the graffitied wall, tracing the symbols in the air with his finger. "You ever hear of the Wemategunis?"

"Weh-mah-what-now?"

"Weh-mah-teh-guh-neese," he said, pronouncing the name like this wasn't the first time he had to spell it out. "Old Lenape word for wood dwarves. They are said to have populated the forests around here in South Jersey, but they've been spotted in Delaware, and parts of eastern Pennsylvania. Haven't heard of them in years. The Hamiltons, the people who used to own this farm before you, never mentioned anything during my pickups."

"I'm sorry, what?"

"Wood dwarves." He said it like I should know this. "Sprites about ye big." He brought his hand to his waist. "Harmless creatures unless you piss them off. You piss 'em off?"

I was too stunned to respond.

"They usually don't bother you. Legend has it, if you don't laugh at their pranks, they can get a smidge aggravated." He stopped eyeing the symbols, then turned back to me. "That, of course, is if the legends are true. You know how it is." He chuckled beneath his breath, then went to work on the clipboard, marking off his sheet. "How many bottles of milk we hauling today?"

"Thirty," I said, still dazed and confused from what he'd just said. I couldn't tell if he was kidding or not. But it all kind of made sense in a strange way. The tripping over my tied shoelaces —shoelaces I, nor my wife, tied together—and the strange symbols. Someone was getting inside locked places, places people could not. "These, uh..."

"Wemategunis," he said again, proud to be able to pronounce the word with such accuracy.

"Yeah, them. Could they, you know, theoretically, get inside the barn if it was locked up?"

He nodded, but not confidently. "Sure. They've been known to operate outside the laws of reality, so I supposed they could get into most places we can't."

"I see..."

"Look," he said, walking over to me. "My advice is—don't mess with them. Just have a laugh, move on. They'll leave you alone if you don't make trouble for them and..."

And what?

"Yes?" I was waiting. Impatiently.

"Just laugh, man." He smiled, but I swore something was hiding behind it, his true feelings about the situation masked behind those curling lips.

Laugh. The cop had told me the same thing. Did he know about this nonsense too? These wood dwarves?

What was I saying? There was no way this was real.

I nodded, told Dave, *Sure thing,* that I'd laugh my ass off about it. Then I handed over the thirty cases of milk and went about my day, never laughing once.

SIX

I purchased the camera equipment and spent all my spare

time that day in the barn setting it up. When I secured the padlock on the barn doors that evening, I felt pretty good about keeping the local hooligans from painting over my wall again. The locks hadn't held them at bay previously, but now that there were cameras mounted on every angle possible (inside and out), there was no way they'd come messing with me.

I was wrong though.

Later that night, about half past midnight, I was wide awake and staring at the monitors I had set up in the office, watching every angle at once. All was quiet on the barn's exterior four sides, and through the white-gray thermal imaging, I couldn't see a single movement coming from within. I just got the sense they were coming back, and so, I couldn't sleep, no matter how hard I tried. I even took some melatonin to lure me to sleep, but every time I shut my eyes I saw those crazy-ass symbols.

Bridge had gone to sleep hours ago, and she was snoring in the other room.

I stared at the monitors, waiting for something to happen. Just when I started to yawn (for maybe the tenth time that hour) and decided that a watched pot never boils, I knew it was time for sleep. I motioned to stand up, and that's when I saw it— movement in the corner of one of the monitors, from the camera in the rear of the barn. It was facing the cow pen, the woods beyond the fencing. I leaned in for a better look. The picture quality was grainy and my eyes strained to take in the image, but within a few seconds, I couldn't deny what I was seeing.

One of *them* was coming.

It trudged forward, moving right past one of the cows. I double-checked to make sure I was recording this, and even fished my phone out of my pocket, just to grab some extra footage in case something happened with the new equipment. I watched as the figure moved forward, taking slow, calculated steps, as if it was expecting a trap ahead.

"I got you, you fucker," I said, not laughing. But maybe I should have.

It walked right up to the camera, right into the field of view, the thermal imaging picking up this small being with such clarity that my heart skipped. It wasn't a kid. If it *was* a kid, they had outdone themselves in the Halloween costume department. The creature (not sure what else to call it at this point) was covered in hair from head to toe, looking more like a small monkey than a human being, though it walked perfectly on two sturdy legs. Like a mini bigfoot. It held something in its hand that looked like a paint bucket. It stopped walking and glanced up at the camera.

Up at me.

My blood froze in my veins. Its glowing eyes burned right into me, and I couldn't shake the feeling it knew I was watching. That it could somehow see through the lens and into my office; like it was staring at me directly. In my eyes. I couldn't detect any hesitance in the creature's movement, no sense of skittishness. It didn't fear me or my tech.

That was maybe the worst of it, losing this game of fear. Having it know I was afraid of it, and I was nothing more to the creature than some inanimate object, something harmless and insignificant.

It tilted its head like it was trying to comprehend my thoughts, and then the camera went out—blinked to black. They all did. Every single one.

Needless to say, I did not sleep that night.

SEVEN

"I don't understand," I told Bridge a few hours later once she was up and getting dressed for school. "I recorded it. And I took video on my camera."

For the hundredth time, I clicked on the video I shot. It played normally, exactly how I filmed it, only it was missing a key component from the original footage—the damn creature. You could see the cow in the background, the fence, the woods beyond, but no goddamn weh-mah-whatchamacallit.

"I believe you, honey," she said in a tone that suggested she didn't believe me, not one bit.

"I swear it happened."

She went back to applying her makeup. I was ready to rip my hair out.

"I need to get some air," I told her, and she told me she loved me.

I went outside and paced the farm, circling the area, looking for footprints, more evidence that this creature had come and trespassed our property in the wee hours. I didn't find footprints, but I found our cows covered in blue paint. All six of them looking like someone had dumped a bucket of house paint over their bodies. Now I know why the thing had been carrying a bucket.

"Jesus Christ," I muttered. The cows didn't seem bothered, but I was already imagining how many hours it would take to lather them with soap and hose them off until they were clean.

Harmless gags.

Just jokes.

Have a laugh.

I could feel my face burning. Maybe it's my fault, maybe it's how angry I get sometimes, but this was a lot—the more time I spent cleaning up these harmless pranks, the less time I had to complete my daily chores, which meant it was costing me money.

Laugh, I thought. *Yeah, right. I'll laugh when they're dead.*

Something in the air changed just then. Not sure what it was, but things felt different. Tasted different. Smelled different.

I didn't think anything of it and headed back to the house.

That's when I heard her scream.

EIGHT

I rushed into the room and saw my wife kneeling on the bed. There were three creatures on the mattress, standing beside her —two of them were holding out her arms, one pulling each limb taught, so hard I thought they were trying to pop the bones out of the sockets. The other one was gripping her forehead with one hand, and the other hand was holding a knife to her throat. Bridge's eyes were wide with absolute terror, and as she wrestled (or tried to; these little hairy dwarves harnessed the strength of ten elephants) with them, screams continued to live and die in her throat.

"Let her go," I demanded, but the little monsters did nothing of the sort.

The one holding the knife growled. *"Luff...et...ooh-es."*

I had no idea what it was saying, but I got down on my knees and clasped my hands together. "Please...let her go. Take me if you have to but leave her alone."

They did nothing of what I asked. They stood there as if waiting for me to respond to something they had said.

Luff et ooh-es.

More of them came out of the bathroom, crawled out from under the bed. I glanced at the window and saw three sets of red eyes beaming back at us. The room smelled like wet horsehide, a bold scent that was causing my stomach to turn. Tears started to burn through my eyes, throwing a bleary shield over the scene in front of me.

"Please..." I said, one last weak attempt to plead with these creatures.

Luff et ooh-es.

I didn't know what it meant.

"Luff et ooh-es," the one behind Bridge spoke again, and for some reason, this time, it clicked.

Laugh at us.

Standing still and remaining silent, they waited for me to respond. The wind roared outside, a gust that caused the old house to creak, the ghostly grind of wood on wood.

Laugh.

Ha.

None of this was funny, not even the harmless gags of tying my shoelaces together and painting my cows blue. Especially not threatening my wife with death.

Bridge begged with her eyes. She wanted me to laugh. Even if I had to fake it.

But I couldn't, couldn't even bring myself to manufacture a gentle smirk.

"Ha," I said, without any hilarity at all. "Ha, ha. Are you satisfied?"

They glared at me with glowing red eyes that I read as, *Not one bit.*

"Let her go, you piece of shit." I was staring at the knife-wielder, my body trembling with anger I never knew I had. I've always had a temper, but this was different. This surging anger knew no bounds, and in about ten seconds, my voice was roaring, and I was punching the end of the bed in front of me. "LET HER FUCKING GO!"

It happened so fast that I had no time to react, to prepare—not that you can for a thing like that.

The wood dwarf dragged the knife across Bridge's throat, opening her like the top of a can of SpaghettiOs. Blood welled in the widening slit, and she began to choke. I was frozen, too stunned to move, but then I realized I had to do something or Bridge was going to die, right there in our bed, just bleed the fuck out.

I rushed forward, but the other two creatures on the bed were there to meet me. They tackled me to the ground with surprising ease—even in my violent panic, I did not possess enough strength to match them, let alone overpower them. They pinned me down and I listened to my wife choke to death on blood and oxygen.

A few blinks after that, they were gone, and I was alone with her.

I couldn't bring myself to look at her body.

So I called the cops. And they came to arrest me.

Isn't that the ultimate gag? I'm currently serving life for a crime I did not commit. All because of my anger. Because I couldn't find the funny in small things.

Ha.

Ha, ha.

THE MARRIAGE

MO MOSHATY

" $\mathcal{I}$ t's only a few hundred more feet, it has to be."

Darren Marsh, stood with his hands on his hips bewildered, feeling every inch of his forty-nine years. Reluctant patriarch-apparent, the only boy child of Hilda and Boris Marsh. Darren had been dragging his feet through the Kummelweck Woods for the last hour and a half, swearing up and down he'd seen the tree line leading to the ancestral family plot at least a dozen times. A journey they took as a family every year since Boris had passed. Every year the 2-mile trek into the dark winding wood would end at the wrought iron gate to the tipping and worn headstones of the Marsh family and Hilda would kneel beside Boris's grave. First it was praying, then, came the swaying. In the last years she'd taken to lying face down on the ground beside it, lifting her head, her ear to the ground, nodding and shaking. The muscles in her neck and body pulled back and forth, by the green and photosynthetic audio of earthen conversations unheard to the others.

Darren would stare off into the distance. The sisters, Agnes, Judith and Andryah, would stand with mouths agape and even in the absence of anyone, felt deeply embarrassed by their mother's actions.

Hilda Marsh was always, by all news, a sane woman. Practical, heritage-woven with all the old wives' tale fuss that comes with coasting a lifetime of knowledge in a wooden boat across the sea. A firm hand and flat tongue. No eyebrows raised in excitement, hands that clapped mildly at entertainment. A curt smile to feign interest. Modest clothing, no crazy patterns, clean lines. Yet here she walked in a bright yellow wool coat with brown leather boots tied up to the knees. A leopard muff and matching hat. She trudged along the footworn path ahead of her children as if pulled along from a heartstring further into the wood. With a stride not seen since they'd been children.

"I feel like we're walking in circles." Andryah, in her thirty-seventh year, was always admonished for her path in life. Free thinker, daddy's girl, wearer of white after Labor Day. The wild progressive at a constant clash with beige Hilda.

"Because we are. She does every year, she gets lost and tries to figure it out. We're gonna get stuck out here and it's already freezing." Agnes, on the cusp of forty-eight, gestured wildly about the woods. She hated these outings. Thirteen years now and no one had said when. No one had declined the invite to this rite of winter. "It's not like she's gonna leave some flowers and have that be that either."

"It has gotten weird, right? What was last year all about? The mumbling. Just nuts." Andryah flicked at the first snowflake on her jacket. "Great."

"This year she'll be speaking in tongues. She's probably got a snake in that muff." Judith, third oldest at forty-four, began to laugh. A mix of mumbled laughter had Darren turn back quickly, just in time to see the woman be smacked by a falling branch.

"Jesus! You guys okay?" Darren ran over.

"Hell no, we're not okay!" Judith had fallen hard to the ground, her long coat covered in mud down the side. Agnes stood pulling twigs out of her hair and Andryah's face was bleeding brightly from a long and deep scratch in her cheek. She was rubbing her head slowly.

"My God." Andryah whispered. They all turned as Hilda stood still, a burst of yellow through the brown-stained forest, looking at them disapprovingly, as she always did. She turned on her heel and kept going.

"Uh mom, could you hang on a damn minute? The hell is wrong with her?" Judith smeared at her coat with the only coffee napkin she had in her possession.

Darren started back up. The look on his mother's face was a cold one, mostly. He had only seen her truly smile and laugh a handful of times, all at his father. There was something about Boris that broke through her exterior. He remembered the roundness and elegance her face took on at those few precious times and at that moment, his mind splintered, juxtaposing her softness to the current angular animal that had stared back at him a minute ago. There was something hard and bitter in her face. He called after her.

Nothing.

Again.

Nothing.

"Mom!" Hilda stopped short, almost sending Darren falling forward as he closed in on her. She placed her hand out onto the wind and traced an imaginary line from left to right. Her eyes closed tight.

"Mom?" He called softly from her right side and then he saw it. A patina of bright greens, ripping texture and coolness. The wrought iron fence.

But he'd have seen it a mile away, he thought.

Hilda took a deep breath and pushed the weathered gate door open and let it sing its aged soprano hymn as it drew its first breath in a year.

Darren glanced behind to find the confused and tired faces of his sisters, trailing up to the gate that had sprung out of left field. Hilda called out to Agnes, eyes fixed on the headstones ahead.

"Agnes, dear, the bag." A light hoarseness in her voice made Agnes's brow furrow. "Here mom." Agnes stepped forward to the left of Hilda and gazed into Darren's eyes in sorrow. Hilda reached behind her with a shaky hand and grasped the burlap bag, clutching it tight to her breast before overturning it on the ground. She fumbled along the ground, pawing, and searching before laying her hands over a small wooden bowl with a jade green inlay.

"Ah. There." Hilda stood quickly and made her way to Boris's headstone and as always, she dropped to her knees in prayer, eyes closed, mouth disjointed, muttering hastily. The snow had begun to interrupt the day as the wind blew in hard from the east. Hilda had thrown her luxurious muff to the ground in her desperate search and now fumbled along the hardened ground at Boris's feet with purpling fingers.

She clasped her hands tight to her chest and let her voice color the enchanted mumblings. A slight gravel in her throat began to croak and it mingled with warm wet tones. Her ramblings were loud now and incoherent. Palms pressed flat to the ground, knuckles pulsing down and up, fingers mauling the ground beneath her.

"Christ! Is she alright?" Andryah gasped and stepped forward, caught short by a cautious Darren.

"Mom, get up!" Agnes shouted into a strong wind as Darren reached out to calm her. "No, Darren, this is crazy!"

Hilda's back arced severely, echoing through the woods like shattered glass. Her mouth now agape in excess, her chin drawing into her chest. Judith screamed and backed away. The others followed. The ground began to quake as the snow pulled in harder causing the siblings to instinctively stand closer.

"The headstones, my God, they're breaking!" Judith pulled away from Andryah's grasp in awe. "Mom, stop it!

The crisp singular flat flakes gave way to stinging needles of ice and wind. The snow began to swallow everything around it. Andryah, Agnes and Judith huddled together as Darren inched slowly in a translucent fog towards the smear of mustard yellow in the wood.

"Mom! Stay where you are! I'm coming!"

Darren lost his footing and slipped near the gate, scraping his hand against a rusted finial. He jerked back splashing blood into the freshly piling snow. The jagged line of crimson began to sink into the snow as if inhaled. Turning his attention to his mother, whose ceaseless state of possession showed no signs of slowing despite the fierce blizzard that surged upon them, his eyes averted to a dim lamplight. It pulsed against the new grey world like an S.O.S.

Darren stepped closer across the hard ground that protested

beneath his feet and tried to discern the origin of this beacon in the wood. Its languid glow hovered above the ground at eye level. Closer still, he moved gently, toe to heel, as if teetering on an invisible tightrope between himself and the luminary spell. A short stop in the wind direction made Darren's eyes grow large at the enormous figure behind the lamplight. Thirty feet in height at the very least, it brushed against a low row of dying evergreens. He turned at a darting flash of yellow.

Hilda's hands were now planted firmly in the ground at the wrists, her arms a twist of saplings and moss. Her eyes were white-glazed, her skin dark and rippled. Her mouth was wide, spilling black and wet clotted dirt onto the ivory ground. She shrieked, piercing the air, and reared her head at a screaming Darren.

Darren continued to scream even after Agnes's hands had pulled him away.

Hilda's body thrashed wildly, trying to dislodge itself from the earth. Spikes of vines entwined and squeezed around her, covering her citrine coat in scratches of brown and green. Guttural shrieks, many voices at once it seemed, parted the wind like a hot knife. And the children stood, helpless, watching their hardened mother be defeated by a lineal landscape.

"What the hell is happening?" Agnes's face dropped as her gaze met the whitened glaze of her mother's eyes. Her heart began to beat in her ears and a single tear formed and fell down her cheek.

"Agnes? Hey! Hey!" Judith moved to shake her. Agnes pushed her away, caught in a daze as her mother twisted, turned, and howled. At what exactly? Darren sat elbows on the ground, unable to move, Judith cried heavily while holding Andryah whose face was buried in her shoulder. Agnes stood watching.

"There's something over there, watching, do you see it?" Darren finally choked the words out after the disbelief eased its grip on his throat. "It's huge. It's got a lantern or flashlight I don't know, but it's watching us."

The sisters fixed their gaze to the left of the iron gate, leaving Hilda undulating against the ground. Judith helped Darren to his feet. Agnes walked slowly ahead of them breaking her gaze on Hilda. She gathered her coat around her face and picked up the pace.

"Agnes, wait for us! You don't know what's out there!" Andryah screamed after her, slipping on the hard-driving snow at her feet. The squall was sideways now, plowing hard into them. The yellow had been all but driven away by the lush green and squalid brown that encircled Hilda.

Agnes stopped short at a large snap. The snap created a sharp groan and a pound to the earth so strong, she lost her footing. She turned behind her, eyes wide, long enough to see Hilda rise from the ground. Twisted skin, bone, and blood puddled to the ground revealing a dark and hardened figure, gnarled beyond repair. The earthen form that had consumed their mother, stood slowly. It swayed in the wind, as tendrils of bark and branch snaked along the snow and pummeled their way in, anchoring the creature.

"Run!" Agnes shouted, reaching back to pull a dazed Darren along.

The creature ultimately broke free and swayed its limbs toward them, shrieking wildly in the driving snow.

The children dashed forward with unreliable footing in as much speed as they could. Judith's face, a stinging stream of tears and dread, Darren, a pallor indistinguishable from the snow. Agnes led the pack, constantly looking over her shoulder at the misshaped ramble of blood and branch. Her mind a jumble of thoughts, her sights set on the glowing lamp light ahead of them.

"Come on!" Agnes shouted to them.

"No!" Darren called. "You don't know what that is!"

Agnes ran faster. The lamp light's fixture began to take on a harder shape. A smooth metal valance with pricks of patina littered its sides and cascaded down to a stone pillar. Agnes stopped tightly. Her mind became hazy, her vision clouded by yellow dust. She dropped to her knees and lifted her head. The heavy din of windy ice drowned out to a soft buzz that crawled through her brain and settled in, stretching, making a home. The buzz gave way to a watery creak and bounced around until it found the word, "Stay."

Agnes stood quickly, almost doubling over again to her knees. She quickly rubbed her snowy hands about her face and took stock of the whereabouts of her siblings. Darren was closing in with Judith close behind.

"You alright?" Darren grasped Agnes's coat tightly. Agnes nodded quickly. Andryah stood steadfast facing the creature. The wind blew through her hair savagely, forming a crude crown about her. The creature was loose now, having snapped its way free of its earthen roots. It moved slowly, calculated, like an animal. Its face, a putrid mix of burgundy tendrils and green spores, a primitive mask of branches anchored by the jowls and jawbone of a once-regal old woman. The jaw dislocated wide and long enough to swallow a small tree and it set its sights on Andryah. It snaked toward her with precision.

"Andryah, come on! Get out of there!" Judith called behind.

She was unmoved. Her fists clenched tightly, drawing blood from her palm onto the snow.

"You hateful bitch! Is this who you really are?" Andryah shouted. "Andryah!! No!" Judith cried after her but was yoked back by Darren.

"Is this what we've come here for? Not for my father! For you! You monster! You killed him, didn't you? Didn't you!" Andryah widened her stance.

Agnes pulled Judith and Darren along.

"We can't leave her!" Darren pushed Agnes away. Agnes walked slowly towards the light, the siblings in shock.

"We have to get her! She's going crazy!" Judith started back down the hill. "You go on ahead. I'm getting out of here." Agnes turned and ran.

"What the hell is wrong with you! It's gonna kill her! Kill us!" Darren turned back at a tiptoeing Judith.

"Judith, no!"

Judith turned back, face red. "But she's all alone."

The creature was lithe, crackling along the ground and in one fell swoop stood tall, grabbing Andryah by her feet and hair and pulling her viciously in two. It dropped her brutishly and shrieked widely at the sky. Andryah's body lay strewn across the porcelain wood, her eyes and mouth wide, frozen in terror. Darren dropped to his knees heaving and vomiting on the ground.

Agnes screamed uncontrollably and Judith fell to the ground unconscious. The creature bounded towards them.

"Darren come on! This way!" Agnes shouted.

Darren wiped his mouth and grabbed onto Judith by one arm, Agnes grappling with the other. Dragging her behind them, the two ran full speed towards the lamp light. As it came into view, they realized the hovering shadow was the flush walls of a stone mausoleum. Running headlong up to the door they dropped Judith's arms and crushed into it. Banging, clawing, kicking, breaking the ornate knobs, and fencing. Agnes's last kick had blown open the door and they rustled inside with Judith, her face soft with oblivion.

They turned at the crackling blare of the creature speeding towards them. Darren carried Judith further into the mausoleum as she began to stir. Agnes stood, shaken, at the door.

Paralyzed by fear, she watched its speed, its agility, its grotesque, hybrid mandible flap wildly in the wind. It pounced toward the mausoleum door and stopped. It stood tall and bounded back down again, pounding its solid and wicked limbs into the ground in anger.

"Close the God damn door! It's going to break its way in! Let's go!" Darren howled to Agnes as he lightly slapped the cheeks of Judith, slowly rousing her.

"I don't think it can." Agnes stepped backward into the stone foyer.

"Oh. Oh God. No!" Judith sat up with a shot, flailing. Darren held her tightly.

"Do you think you could come over here for a minute, Agnes! Christ!" Darren and Judith began to cry. Agnes stood solid.

"I heard something before it charged us."

"That thing? Is that her?" Darren gently released Judith. Judith sidled along the wall, peeking her head out of the doorway just enough to wince back in. "God. What is she?"

"Did you hear it? Either of you? It said something." "Hear what? What did it say?"

The wind bellowed through the open crypt doors, slamming them shut. The odd buzz was back, dancing at its post between Agnes's ears. A strong musk of rot and greenery took hold in the small foyer and enveloped the three in terror. They slowly huddled together as the creaks and slow crunching of branches weaved its way between the wind and the shrieks of the creature.

The creaks ploddingly made their way into a cadence. One, two. One, two. Over and over. Growing ever closer, pushing the three together just the same. The source, Darren had discovered, was positioned at the left end of the foyer. Two vertical rows of entombed Marsh

men and women parted from the rest only by a small, rounded archway door. On the other side lay four more rows of Marsh's stacked five high. The door opened with a crack and smack of wind. A familiar voice rang out.

"It said, stay."

Judith screamed and covered her ears. She knelt on the stone floor rocking back and forth.

"Dad?" Darren spoke softly, choked again by disbelief.

Boris Marsh stood before them, as knotted and twisted as

Hilda. Deep mahogany skin, flecked by moss eaten divots. His face pulled to either side of his head, sappy bark emerging from beneath.

"Don't be frightened. I'm so glad you've come."

Judith continued to scream and back away. Agnes moved closer.

"We had no choice but to come here." Agnes said indignantly. "It was chasing us. What happened to her. Why is she like this?"

Boris spoke, his voice jagged and hoarse, like an old wooden boat mingling with the tide. "She is what she wanted to become. She knew the risks of defying tradition. Of stopping centuries of institution. Of blood. Of obedience."

"But you're dead. Are we crazy? Are we going crazy? What the hell is going on?" Judith clutched against the wall in terror.

"What tradition?" Darren swallowed hard.

"Every Marsh that has ever lived, was born, or has sailed across any ocean to lay roots down, has Leshy running through its blood. Every cell, every muscle, alive with the power to suck the life out of anything that comes across them. Your mother knew this, knew all the found forces I was held to, what she would be held to because she loved me. Until she didn't."

"What forces?" Agnes said flatly.

"To bear the weight of a wooden soul, perhaps. It's a long road, marriage. The give, the take, the permissions you ask for and give, the roles you lead and the life you leave behind.

Choosing me, choosing to be a Marsh, well, Hilda knew all to well that would be everlasting. Planning to leave me was never part of the equation."

"Are you saying, she wanted to leave you?" Judith chimed from a distant corner of the foyer.

"In a matter of speaking. She wanted to end the curse on her, on all of you."

"What curse?!" Darren was charging now, at what he had no idea, and slowed his pace to sidle up next Agnes.

Boris stepped forward. The children lined up against the rows of Marsh family tightly, afraid. Boris faced them solidly and opened the mausoleum door. The creature wailed and shrieked and tossed its body about violently.

"Do you see her? This is what she was always running from. Killing me wouldn't solve it. Residing, breeding, laying with Leshy, it comes at a price. She was worth everything to me."

"Dear God." Darren gasped. "Killing you?" Darren turned hard to Agnes.

"So, she did do it." He whispered. "I can't handle this."

"You will have to handle it Darren, last of my name. You see, your mother, is not the woman she once was."

"She killed Andryah!" Judith snapped.

"Andryah was doomed. Who do you think helped her do it? It was no loss to your mother, I'm sure. But I should have known." Boris looked longingly at the creature. "I should have known I couldn't trust her to remain obedient. To continue the legacy. A fool I was, to believe the lies of a Vedmak's daughter. And I thought, I thought I could change her mind. Every year she's come to curse me. Every year she's come to undo the burden laid upon my name. For you! But look! Look at what she's made me do! She is powerless to fight tradition."

Boris yelled and cackled in the doorway, his voice getting lost beyond the door by the howling wind.

"We're not like you! We're human! Her blood runs through our veins too!" Agnes shouted.

Boris's tendrils in his hands broke free, lashing at Agnes's wrist, Judith's arm, and Darren's face.

"You think you can outrun tradition! Look! Feel!"

Judith pressed into her wound, her eyes widened as she felt around the sinew and into the rough and scratchy bark, she grasped onto something slippery and pulled it out slowly. A single leaf. She slid down the wall in silence. Darren's check hung open like a popped balloon, smooth wispy branches moved gingerly inside of it. The color drained from his face.

"I tried to tell you. I tried to show you so many times. My children." Boris's makeshift lips splintered as he spoke. "She brought you here to dangle in my face and lock me out with her incantations and her hocus-pocus and her spasms. Keeping me from you, keeping you safe. Safe from all this. But I have her now. She can't escape all of us."

Darren's eyes in a loving embrace of a purple ring, sunken. Drained. His chest shallow, barely breathing. Judith rocked silently.

"You see Agnes. Everyone is coming along. Let's see."

Boris's tinder fingers clasped around Agnes's wrist. He inspected her wrist and dropped her arm suddenly.

"No! No! Where is it! Where is our legacy?" Boris howled.

Agnes inspected her open wrist, her focus waning. Nothing but blood and fresh, wet, puffy fat patches. Agnes bolted out of the open doors towards the creature. The creature threw its head back and shrieked, snatching Agnes quickly and sprinted through the woods outrunning Boris's moan. Agnes's blood sprinkled a light trail behind them. She blinked twice before the blackness swallowed the world.

Agnes awoke slowly. She was warm, a low light of a fire in a fireplace. She let her eyes dart around a while before settling on a familiar face.

"Ah, you're awake." Hilda smiled. "What happened?"

Hilda sighed. Her eyes pink, her wrists bound with bandages.

"Something I should've let happen a long time ago. I held onto them as best as I could." "I know mom. But Andryah."

Hilda began to sob.

"She had turned against me long ago. I had no choice."

Agnes sat up. She held onto Hilda's hand gently and stroked it. "So, what now?"

"Well. We start over. Anywhere." "I'd like that." Agnes smiled.

"Me too." Hilda tapped her on the leg through the heavy Afghan blanket.

"Mom?"

"Did you use any incantations on me?" Agnes laid back into bed.

"Yes. The same one my mother used on me. No man forged against you shall prosper."

FEATHER
BRET NELSON

avid Relton was running behind. He was expected at the stone circle before midnight, with the six heads he'd carry in the ancient, grey haversack. So far, he'd prepared only three.

Last summer's offering went easier. Now, his elbows made popping noises. His eyes burned. And this mountain air felt so thin. Were these oblations heavier? Or maybe his age made the work harder.

The witch had made him a promise. This was Relton's thirty-ninth year in her service, and tonight's duties would be the last in his current form.

If he was prompt.

She must have arrived at the stones by now. She'd be starting her preparations.

He had allowed himself five hours for the cutting and cleanup — all finished by eleven. Here it was nine-thirty and two heads to go after this one. Then he still had to tidy the site.

After everything was hidden away, after all his footprints and drag marks were eliminated, he'd strain to carry the haversack back to the truck. Then it was a four-mile drive to the hill. Then another mile on foot, with the sack, to meet the witch at the stones.

He needed to catch up. But every time he got a good rhythm going the damn saw would catch on the down stroke, sending dull sparks of pain through his arm. Earlier, he lost his grip on the handle and the blade nearly tore into his thumb.

The hacksaw was brand new and keen, so he couldn't blame the tool. This man, this delivery driver, had a solid neck. Dense layers of tendons stretched in all directions. The saw didn't have any grain to cut with or against.

The driver must have gone to the gym every day.

Relton's allergies ramped up. The pines made his head feel tight as he forced the tool to stay in its groove.

———

The Angeles National Forest was twenty miles north of Hollywood, and it held more secrets than even that town could imagine. Relton had been to this clearing many times before, but it kept itself hidden. The surrounding woods grew at an unnatural rate.

Still, he found the way. Earlier, he drove his truck through the correct break in the pines. He knew which of the fire-scarred trees to follow, leading him to the place at the bramble's edge where he could park. He knew where to find the gap in the bramble, overgrown but passable, where the hiking path was revealed.

That path led to the clearing. It was quiet there, like most of the places where evil surged. An old, two-room cabin leaned to the north, a few yards inside the tree line. A wide, primeval stump stood nearby, with chopped firewood piled to one side.

There were no tire tracks, no footprints. Spiders claimed ownership of the woodpile years before. It looked like no one had been here for ages.

But some of her thralls had been here earlier today.

Behind the cabin, just where they were supposed to be, Relton found two large tarps, each covering a shape a little smaller than a queen-size bed. The tarps were tied, staked, and tucked up neatly with a five-inch berm of quicklime surrounding them, keeping hungry animals and bugs away. Gear was stacked between the tarps, all of it new: A ladder, a cart, six coolers, and a large, plastic bin with tools, rags, rope, and the like.

Each tarp covered three recent dead, making six oblations in all. Their eyes were open. Their feet pointed southwest. Their hands were bound with sackcloth.

Perfect.

He didn't know who was tasked with this delivery, but they had excelled in their service.

How could he make up the time?

The first three heads came free with little effort. His work was efficient and clean.

He felt good about it, complimenting his own progress. With a momentary flash of ego, he had forgotten his place. Relton was subservient to a solitary witch. His progress was hers to judge.

So now, the dark energies slowed him down. A reminder to keep his thoughts centered on her needs. But he had to make this work. She would keep her word if he fulfilled his obligations. Nothing else mattered.

Bubbles formed between his fingers on the saw's handle. Earlier, it kept getting slick with blood, so he wrapped a rag around the grip. Now the rag kept getting sopped, had to be wrung out. More stops and pauses.

Relton focused on keeping his strokes long and even. At least he didn't have to dispose of the bodies anymore.

The cabin belonged to one of the witch's associates, a skinny cannibal named Aldo Kerr. Decades ago, he gave himself the title, "Der Mumienmacher." Relton spent more time than he cared to remember in that cabin, assisting Kerr in the creation of corpse medicines. The process lasted for days. Every hour, the air grew thicker with the heat and odors of the foul work.

First, Relton sectioned the cadavers while Kerr, mad on amphetamines, yelled at him in German. The organs were preserved in salt, whole. A clandestine Anthropophagus Cult in Santa Monica always needed them and paid top dollar. Frequently, the witch ordered Relton to make the deliveries, and he was always invited to stay and sample. He didn't want to, but the witch told him not to be rude.

Next, they'd extract the fat. The steam and smells from the vats stole Relton's breath. He spent hours stirring the slurry until all but the lipids boiled away. Once cooled, it looked like shortening from the grocery store. Kerr sealed the cleanest portions in clay jars labeled "ARMSUNDERFETT." The rest became thieves' candles and liniments.

Finally, anything left of the cadavers was mummified, then powdered. This skill set Kerr apart from his competitors. Mummy Powder was a rare commodity.

Of course, the mummification process was the most demanding of all. And after the drug-fueled, sleepless days, Kerr's pupils constricted to pinpoints as his mind seethed. He often turned violent. More than once Relton had to flee.

Then, on the witch's orders, he had to return. And apologize.

A few years ago, the cannibal took on an apprentice. He was a much younger man with far stranger tastes. The last time Relton saw them, they were each missing two fingers. He didn't inquire, that would be rude.

————

Something moved among the pines. A new, heavy sound. Quick, circling. Had one of the victims survived?

He turned to the big tree, where his headlamp revealed the nurse and the artist. They were still suspended by their ankles, the holes in their necks draining blood into the coolers he'd be leaving for Kerr.

Movement again, this time to his right. And a chittering sound. Could it be one of her homunculi, come to check his progress?

A few taps made the lamp brighter as Relton tracked the sound. Near the cabin, he found the culprit, a raccoon. The creature was probably curious about these strange smells of quicklime, sweat, and blood. Once exposed, it regarded the scene for a few more seconds, then scampered off.

Relton found a clean spot on his sleeve and wiped his eyes again. "Should have brought goggles," he thought. Tiny pops of blood were all over him. They kept hitting his eyes. "Don't think about it, just keep ... working ... the ... blade."

———

During his earliest years of service, the witch assigned him to Emilia Navarro, her shaper. There were people who loved the witch profoundly, and they wished to be more than thralls. Navarro worked her craft on them.

She altered these most devoted followers. They became the witch's homunculi.

It was the ultimate demonstration of their adoration. Salves were massaged on and below their skin to make their bones and joints malleable. They drank pliability tinctures to help their organs slide into new positions as the work progressed.

Some of them were bound to elongation lattices. Over several months, the horizontal gears ratcheted wider, altering their ligaments and condyles, creating hypermobility.

Others were inched into porcelain molds, pressing them into new forms.

A few spent a year inside a series of smaller and smaller compression boxes, making their statures more portable.

Wide leather tourniquets made heads cylindrical or flat.

Relton spent his days suspending weights, turning rods, and tightening straps.

By the time they left the shaper's care, these people had become the most exotic of pets.

———

He couldn't feel his fingers anymore, but he kept the blade moving.

The haversack was already heavy with only three heads. This one, if he ever managed to cut it loose, would probably weigh more than any pair of them. It would be a great burden, getting them all to the stones.

"Twelve pounds each by six makes sixty, no, seventy-two pounds," he thought. "Gonna be a long walk up that hill."

Were their brains important? He could scoop them out easily enough. She had made it clear the expressions were critical. It was imperative their eyes were open and features unchanged from the moment they crossed into death.

That meant the skulls were important, so the faces held their shapes. That meant the teeth and tongues were important, so the mouths wouldn't tilt. But rigor froze the expressions, so the brains were not important, and they were three or four pounds each.

His thoughts were happily interrupted as the saw came through the back side of the neck and the head fell to the towel below. The lantern on the ground nearby revealed the tiniest, satisfied smile on the delivery driver's face. Nothing like the frozen scream on the last one, that old man with the beard.

———

Twenty years ago, a man of great wealth made a bargain with the witch. Charles Girard offered her an ancient conjuring drum in exchange for four favors. The witch agreed to the trade, as Girard had unknowingly asked for trivial charms. She delivered on all of them within a week.

But the drum she received was a high-quality fake. And Girard knew it, as he was the one who ordered its fabrication. She let him believe he had outsmarted a clever witch. Then, she hexed him. "He will know ruin," she said.

She required three components for the hex, and Relton was tasked with getting them. It was the first time she had given him a duty to perform alone.

He'd have to gather writing by Girard's hand, a scrap from one of his meals, and a newly cut lock of his hair. These things had to come from inside his home.

The witch assured Relton he would not be seen. She'd make him a shadow. The spell would take hold at midnight and the enchantment would last for twenty-four hours.

So, at midnight, he was outside Charles Girard's security gate. He knew the time; he'd been checking his watch constantly. Yet, he saw the watch. Looking at his hands and body, he could see every inch of himself.

The witch told him this would be so, that his eyes would capture his own presence, but to everyone else, he'd be invisible. He was to enter the house through the front door. It would not be locked, and no alarm would sound.

For a moment, he wondered if he'd upset her. Some slight? Was this vengeance? Would he be shot by a homeowner's pistol?

No matter. He was bound to her will. From the front porch, he looked back along the driveway to the tall gate. He didn't remember getting past it. The door swung open as he reached for the handle. It closed once he stepped inside the house. He saw himself in the mirrored walls of the entrance hall, but when he came into the study, neither Girard nor his dog took any notice.

After the man went to bed, Relton pulled tiny scissors and an envelope from his pocket. He cut a lock of Girard's hair and tucked it away. The snip echoed through the room, but neither Girard nor his young wife stirred. Relton stood next to the bed for the rest of the night, watching them sleep.

The morning came, and Relton remained unseen by the couple. He trailed them both, saw the secrets they hid from each other. The foul images Girard kept in a hidden file case. The tiny cuts his wife made under her thigh.

Though all three of the witch's hex components were gathered before noon, Relton stayed in the house until just before midnight. He took pleasure from it. And the witch never gave him such an assignment again.

The old man's head in the haversack, the one with the frozen scream, belonged to Charles Girard. He was still in his prison jumpsuit.

———

With care, Relton wrapped the driver's head in silk and put it with the others. He rolled the remains off the stump and onto the cart, then returned the body to its original spot behind the cabin, recreating the groupings as he had found them.

Relton pulled the cart to the tree where the nurse and the artist waited. He stretched his back and shoulders, holding his hands together and reaching up high. "I'll save four pounds per if I can get those brains out," he thought, "But that damn optic nerve."

With his foot, he closed the cooler under the nurse and pushed it out of the way. Looking up to position the ladder, his ears pounded from the allergies. "These damn pines."

As he cut the nurse down, he watched the hole in her neck. She'd been hanging by her ankles for more than an hour and she was still bleeding a little. "Should've brought goggles."

She dropped and he wheeled her to the stump. The cart's large, balloon tires moved well over the uneven ground. He felt a growing appreciation for it and thought, for a moment, about how much easier his work would be if he used the cart to haul the haversack back to the truck.

No. Bearing the burden was a component of his trial. The sack would only move if it were on his shoulders.

———

One week ago, the witch verified his assignment. "Thrall Relton, your part in this is crucial. The Beast's tithe is six heads," she said. "The oblations will be found in the usual place. You will remove their heads and bring them to the stones. You will lay them at my feet.

"Each must hold the face of their passing; their expressions must be as a portrait painted." The command was as it always had been. The same words, the same inflection.

Around the room, her homunculi were in constant motion. The thin one rolled from under the chaise, giggled, then somersaulted to a perch at the window. Another used its extra knees and elbows to cling to the tall column behind her chair.

It slid down the column and stopped when it reached her shoulder. Once there, its cylindrical head rotated until its mouth reached the witch's ear.

It whispered to her.

She nodded. "Yes, pet. Yes, I remember our promise to Thrall Relton."

David Relton felt his heart race as she spoke to him. "For thirty-nine years you have served me, that is thrice thirteen. After this task is complete, you'll soar for me. You'll ride the thermals of drifting souls."

She walked to him and took his hand. "You will have a new, dark form. For me, you will carry. And fetch."

He hadn't dare mention it, hadn't dare hope. But she said it aloud. Her promise would be made real, and nothing else in the world mattered.

———

A deep sniff brought no relief to Relton's stuffed sinuses. "These pines," he said. He pulled a flask from his pocket and took a sip of apple juice that became a big swallow that became a chug that spilled down his chin. He wiped his face with a fresh rag, then wrapped it around the hacksaw's handle and stretched his back again.

He nudged the nurse with his hip, shifting her to a better position on the stump. She lay on her back, looking skyward. He drew the blade across her neck five times, forming a deep slot to guide the cutting. Then the push and pull began.

He wondered how the oblations were dispatched this year. Did they die nearby? Or under the tarp? Did their lives end in an instant, leaving a snapshot of what they were feeling on their faces? Or were these expressions a reaction to their passing, perhaps their first acknowledgment of what they experienced on the other side?

Already, he felt the blade gnawing at the nurse's spine. This one was going faster. The tempo carried his mind back to the optic nerves, to the puzzle he'd been trying to solve. "Without the brains, the sack's gonna be twenty or thirty pounds lighter," he thought. "But the damn nerve ties the brain to the eyes."

The witch required those expressions. And if he tugged on those nerves, it might move the eyes. Who could say what odd things might happen if the eyes shifted around? No, it wasn't worth the risk.

The nurse's chin lifted a little higher with each stroke of the saw. Her head would drop soon. Every move he made ratcheted his aches. His elbow made that popping sound on every other stroke. But it didn't matter. He was back on schedule.

He'd lay these heads at her feet and offer to help arrange them on the glyphs among the stones. She might let him watch as she danced. With his promises kept, she'd keep hers. A gift for his thirty-nine years of service.

The witch would remake him. He'd witnessed that long, excruciating process before. She said he wouldn't remember it.

In time, his fresh bones would harden, his changed muscles would become strong. Then, he'd soar, for her.

At last, he'd know joy when he became her falcon.

the
SPIDER
and her parlor

MOCHA PENNINGTON

She could hear their conversation from the living room. Bits and pieces at first, just tiny fragments that had chipped away when their voices rose above a whisper. Blane and Troy didn't possess the ability to mask any conversation in discreet tones for too long. Their voices were heavy, whispers always crushed and murdered under their weight eventually.

Their voices were amplified as they swept through the barren house; their laughter harsh and sharp, like the threat of a blade held upon her throat. They had been like this since childhood, their secrets penetrating the dense cloak of night and always managing to find her ears. Sumner had accumulated years' worth of unwanted details about her brother and Troy. She had a special section of her mind devoted to their discussions. She knew all their impish acts, their crushes and rivals, and, on a few occasions, the breathy pants from the experiments they conducted on each other in their late teens.

They didn't speak of anything incriminating now, just their typical, crass talk of women who they found physically appealing. Their Airbnb hostess was the subject of the current discussion, who they nicknamed Snow White.

"...hair as black as ebony, skin as white as snow and lips as red as blood," Blane said.

"I think it's 'lips red as a rose'," Troy corrected.

They laughed then, their words crippled by their mirth.

Sumner couldn't recall their hostess' name, but she *was* gorgeous, and rightfully earned the nickname Snow White, especially when considering her complexion. It was smooth like porcelain, and white, shockingly so. It was almost *too* white as if her blood ceased to circulate some time ago. Her hair was black, thick and glossy, falling in soft layers to the heart of her breasts. It was beautiful hair but did no favors to add warmth to her pale complexion.

She had been waiting for them in the living room when they arrived yesterday. She smiled at their surprise when finding her there. It had been a disarming smile, her teeth even and nearly as white as her skin. Her willowy figure had been dressed in a black pencil skirt and a gray silk blouse, both the neckline of the blouse and the length of her heels wanted to be seen as sophisticated but not a total bore. Her lips and fingernails were the same color of red, a red that appeared as though she had painted them in blood.

"I didn't mean to startle you," she said. Her voice was smoky with a noticeable rasp. It was a voice that could make reading off a grocery list sound seductive. "I just wanted to greet you all and make sure you have everything you need." There was a hint of an accent somewhere too, barely clinging to her words. Perhaps it was a watered-down English accent, or maybe it was one from up north, Boston or New Jersey? Or it might have been an amalgamation of several—the accent of a well-traveled person.

Blane introduced himself, then Troy, Troy's girlfriend, Jela, and finally Sumner. The woman shook their hands at each introduction, a slight discomfort crossing their faces as she did. Sumner was unsure why until the woman took her hand into hers. Her skin was impossibly cold as if winter retreated there at the start of spring. It was a cold that seeped into your skin and bit.

"I can give you a tour while I'm here," she had said, spinning around with the grace of a ballerina before polite protest could be issued. Blane and Troy followed eagerly, like puppies scared to be alone. She brought them through the living room, describing it as minimalistic; but to Sumner, it looked empty and sad, the sleek furnishings shrouded in a palette of dark hues brought to mind a person who treated their depression in stylish clothing.

Sumner couldn't remember most of what their hostess had said during the short tour. She had been captivated by her, maybe a little envious. She carried herself with the air of a woman who knew she was beautiful and had grown bored of being told so.

"My living quarters are downstairs in the basement," she had said after the tour, "be as loud as you wish, don't trouble yourself by walking on eggshells. I'm fine with noise. If you need anything or have questions, do call me. My number is on a Post-it by the landline. You are, by no means, to come downstairs."

Her last sentence conjured a chill to haunt the room. A threat had been buried in her words, a threat that couldn't be softened by her smile.

"Why would someone *choose* to live in the basement of a house?" Jela had whispered at their hostess' departure. "That's weird."

"Who cares?" Blane said, "she's hot."

"Oh, definitely," Troy concurred. "Ten outta ten, for sure."

A scowl had marred Jela's features. "Well, I don't like her," she pouted, crossing her arms about her chest.

Sumner had lain in bed that night with her thoughts turned to that curious woman and her quiet threat.

You are, by no means, to come downstairs, she had said. Those words were on a continuous loop in her head, her tone becoming more ominous and less human with each lap.

Her curiosity was piqued. Images of what was shuttered behind the basement door weaved themselves through her mind, in time with the dark rhythm of the woman's voice. They were of macabre images, a torrent of them; images of severed body parts, upholstery made of skin, dishes fashioned from bone. Walls painted in splatters of blood, human meat decaying in cracks of floorboards, maggots pouring from—

Sumner set up in bed, breathless, those terrible images leaving a dark stain on her mind. Blane stirred at her movement. He mumbled something inaudible before settling back into slumber. She stared at his profile awash in shadows to be sure he was completely submerged in sleep.

She then sighed, breaking apart the grimy residue those images had left.

She hadn't shared a bed with him since they were kids. She had forgotten how light of a sleeper he was. She wanted to be home in her own bed, a bed where the right side had remained cold for a century, it seemed. She wasn't supposed to be a part of their trip to Denver. She was a last-minute replacement after Blane and his girlfriend finally split after four toxic months together. The flights, Airbnb and activities had already been booked and paid for. "All you gotta do is show up," Blane had told her, his brown eyes full of plea edged in sadness.

The memory was dissolved by a not-so-distant sound. Footsteps, she translated it as, footsteps and...something else. She held her breath and forsook any movement as she listened. It sounded as if something heavy yet soft was being dragged along with whoever owned those delicate footfalls.

Who owned those footsteps!? Her mind had screamed at her.

She thought of Jela, creeping off to the sofa after a poisonous, late-night quarrel with Troy, a dense blanket dragging behind her. But Jela's flare for dramatics had no room for stealth, and if she were miserable, she demanded company. It couldn't have been Troy either. His feet, much like his voice, were heavy. His tiptoeing would still rattle windows in their frames.

She had listened more intently then, a cast of cold fright overlaying her skin when realizing those footsteps were moving closer, toward her and Blane's room.

A scent wafted into the room as those footsteps grew nearer. It was a horrid, sharp smell, a nauseating odor of vinegar, dirt and death, but not the death of any mammal, it was the death of something else entirely.

The footfalls stilled right at the threshold. The door was a little more than ajar, giving a tease of what stood in the shadows. Sumner couldn't breathe; her heart played a frantic tune at her chest, an aggressive, metal ballad with enough force to shatter her bones.

She had made out a slender arm, its whiteness luminous against the sinister depth of darkness surrounding it. Something was working its way past the door and into the room. It was a timid approach as if it were testing the water before wholly submerging. She believed it had been a hand at first, but it was too thick to be a hand, and it had no fingers, no wrist. It was cylinder in shape, tapering off to a...*claw*? Was it covered in hair —thick, dark hair? She could hear those hairs scraping along the wood to the door.

What the fuck is that!? Her mind panicked, unable to translate what it saw. She then caught her mind's chaotic disease. She might have screamed then or gasped so loud it sounded like a scream. Her body was emancipated from the chokehold of fear had had on it. She clambered to the end table and switched on the lamp, knocking it to the floor in her haste. Half the room filled with distorted, saturated light.

"What are you *doing*?" Blane asked, his voice tight with sleep and irritation.

Sumner could only jut her finger at the door, terror stiffening the movement. Whatever had been there was gone, the phantom of its horrible scent lingering in the air.

———

Sumner sat up in bed now, the horror of last night clinging to her mind like stubborn cobwebs. She didn't know when she was able to drift off to sleep last night, but she had gripped to the thought that maybe, when she woke, the memory would be faded and worn like an elusive dream, circling the drain of her subconscious.

She could hear the upstairs shower running when she entered the living room, which was probably why Troy spoke so boldly of their Airbnb hostess—Snow White, she decided she would call her—with abandon.

"There's some coffee in the maker," Blane told her. "We used all the cream, so you'll have to take yours black."

"Just like your mom takes her dick!" Troy couldn't help but to jest.

Blane laughed. "Yeah, I walked right into that. But Black and Mexican is a good mix, *your* mom can vouch for *that*."

They erupted into laughter while Sumner poured herself coffee. They always could joke with ease, knowing each other's boundaries without being told. She supposed over a decade of friendship could do that. She found herself wondering what would become of them if they had allowed their experimentations to go beyond silent experiences.

She suddenly smelt that awful odor from last night. It reached across the kitchen, encompassing her with noxious tentacles, souring the swig of coffee in her mouth. She scowled at the smell. Her gaze fell to the basement door not far from where she stood at the kitchen counter.

You are, by no means, to come downstairs.

She took small, cautious steps toward it, the odor becoming more pungent as she did. She moved as if she were summoned, her control lost, her body no longer her own. The odor was the strongest right at the door. It was a dense, unbearable odor that added weight to her lungs. And was there a presence on the other side, a grinning presence that found delight in her disobedience? She thought so. If she listened closely, she could almost hear its breathing, heavy and serrated. Surely it was an unkind imagination that conjured such vivid details. Her hand, trembling, was reaching for the knob.

"God, I *needed* that!" Jela called out, walking down the stairs. Her voice stole Sumner's attention, breaking a spell she hadn't known she was under. As she journeyed down the steps, Jela's skin was given a sheen when it caught the light, still damp from the thick moisturizer she'd lathered on.

"You're better then?" Troy asked.

"A hundred times better," Jela answered, blowing out her cheeks in a sigh. She ran her fingers through her curls that had recently been cut close to her scalp and were bleached and toned to an ashy blonde. The cut, Sumner thought, gave prominence to her high cheekbones and lent an edge to her beauty.

"What happened?" Sumner asked, moving into the living room.

Jela smiled, thrilled to be under a momentary spotlight. "That woman must have a dog or something," she said, "I woke up covered in hair. It was itchy as hell. I thought I'd never get it off."

"It's weird," Troy added, "we didn't even see any hair when we got into bed last night." He shrugged. "Must've been stuck to the blanket."

"Well, I *will be* mentioning this in my Yelp review," Jela said.

As the three dove into a facile conversation, Sumner's thoughts drifted to last night. She could almost hear the dreadful song of coarse hair rubbing against wood. Denial, frantic and swift, intervened with the truth, mangling it. *You were half asleep*, denial told her, its voice weak, unconfident, *it wasn't real.*

What had been trying to stealthily work itself into the room then? It had to have been a limb of some sort, or an appendage even, with thick hair sprouting from it. Had it gone upstairs after she dozed off? And something was familiar about that pale arm she had seen too. The familiarity of it nagged at her, half her brain wanted her to see something the other half refused to acknowledge.

Perhaps it was for the best?

They spent the day in the Rocky Mountains, a location they would spend most of their time in Denver at. Today was a six-hour hike/tour, tomorrow they were scheduled for rafting, and then they were to go zip lining on their final day. Sumner wasn't sure if any fun could be had with Jela's incessant complaining.

They had barely been on the trail for thirty minutes when the complaints began. They were small at first, humorous even, eliciting polite chuckles and smiles from those on the trail with them. But the smiles and chuckles vanished as her complaints became more frequent, more verbose. They separated themselves from her, even Blane and Troy walked serval feet ahead, leaving Sumner to be Jela's accomplice in misery.

"Troy and Blane like all this outdoorsy shit, not me," Jela ranted, wiping sweat from her forehead. "I should've backed out coming when Blane and Sasha broke up. She was the only reason I agreed to come. Why couldn't they just stay together until *after* this trip?"

Sumner frowned. "I mean...she hit him because his ex-girlfriend *liked* one of his Instagram pictures."

Jela, in reply, smacked her lips and tossed her eyes skyward. "It'll be different if *he* hit *her.*"

Sumner wanted to argue that the gender of the aggressor shouldn't play any role in the severity of domestic violence but chose not to. Arguing with someone who quarreled as a hobby would never have a productive outcome. She kept her silence and slowly caught up with Blane and Troy.

She didn't think about last night's incident until their rental drove onto the mile-long strip of lone road leading to their Airbnb. The house was part of a cul-de-sac kept tucked away and out of reach behind a gate.

Blane exited the driver's seat to punch in a code, and the gate rolled open. Sumner half expected Jela to complain about the gate and the inconvenience it was, but Jela held all comments to herself, quietly sulking in the backseat. Jela and Troy had gotten into an argument sometime after the hike had concluded.

Her silent treatment was a gift to them all.

The cul-de-sac was U-shaped with two houses on the left, two on the right and one at the center, which belonged to their hostess. It was a quaint house of white stone and black trim, a charming house at first glance but blanketed you in unease the closer you looked. Sumner felt that unease now, more so than she had yesterday when first arriving. It was the prickling knowledge that something shared the house with Snow White that sent her unease into overdrive.

It's just your imagination; nothing is in that house, denial told her through clenched teeth.

"Do they watch everyone who comes through the gate, or just us?" Blane asked, amused.

Sumner noticed slight gaps in curtains and blinds from the surrounding houses, where an observer stood, their identity concealed in distance.

"If we wake up to hooded figures and a burning cross in the front lawn, then I'm gonna ask for a full refund," Troy said.

Jela and Troy went upstairs when they entered the house, surely to unleash the hostile tension that had been building between them most of the day. Blane declared a nap was much needed after hiking for so long and went to their shared room. Sumner was left alone in the living room. wondering if the other three were too preoccupied to make note of the stench hovering like a cloud in the room.

Maybe it is *your imagination*, she thought, seating herself on the uncomfortable sofa. She reached for the remote on the glass table, hoping to come across a marathon of *Love & Hip-Hop* or *Basketball Wives* on VH1. Her attention was stolen by something on the floor. She aborted the remote, leaned over and plucked a strand of hair from the floor. The hair was about an inch or two long, and it was thick, much thicker than a dog's. *Thick and strong*, she mused, bending it in between her fingers.

She wondered what sound would be made if a limb covered in hairs like the one she held was rubbing against a wooden doorframe. *Much like the one I heard last night?* She let the hair fall from her fingers to be lost from sight.

———

Sumner jolted awake, later that night, her chest tight with panic and something was on the tip of her tongue. It might have been words gathering there, ready to blunder from her mouth the moment it opened. Or it could have been a scream, clawing itself to liberation.

Did she have a bad dream, one that stalked her to wakefulness, only to linger in the shadows to be felt but not remembered? She couldn't say. She did know something was wrong. The house seemed to know this too. It held its breath, all sound absorbed into its walls. A dark tingle of anticipation crawled along her skin as she listened to the house's deep silence.

And then movement.

A series of dull thumps and creaking floorboards tore through the dense silence with savage teeth. Sumner clapped her hand over her mouth, murdering a gasp. They had to be coming from the stairs, those thumps. And they weren't the chaotic melody of a fall. A method was in their rhythm. Something heavy was being dragged carefully down the stairs, she realized. Another sound was woven with the thumps and delicate footfalls: The gentle scrape of coarse hair against its surroundings.

That dreadful harmony of sounds ceased for just a moment as if it were listening to Sumner the same way she was listening to it. Then it resumed, not down the stairs but on the floor, the thumps replaced by the long sigh of something large being pulled against the smooth hardwood flooring.

As the sound lessened by distance, Sumner debated if she should have a peak from the bedroom door to see what was happening. Curiosity surged through her like adrenaline, urging her to move, but fear kept her rooted in place. Curiosity and fear had a heated argument inside her, and she wasn't aware which became the victor until she was unlocking the bedroom door she had locked before going to bed.

That hideous odor struck Sumner like a slap once the door was open. It thickened the air like a presence. She could nearly feel that odor laying on her skin, entering her body with each breath. She could even taste it at the back of her throat, churning the contents of her stomach.

She grimaced as she moved through the odor on the tips of her toes, her heart pounding, desperate not to make a sound. A door closed once she made her way into the living room, and the thumps returned, muffled this time, and decreasing in volume the farther they traveled downward. Sumner didn't have to give any thought to where those thumps might be headed. She quickened her pace to the door leading to the kitchen.

At the door, she was able to just barely hear one final thump before the dragging sound returned. And then nothing. The house released its breath, giving back the faint, electrical hum of the appliance's voices. They seemed to be whispering to each other, gossiping about what they had just witnessed.

———

"...fucking ridiculous," Jela hissed the next morning, yanking Sumner from sleep.

"He might need to just cool off," Blane replied, his voice reassuring.

Sumner pulled herself from bed and went to the living room. Blane and Jela were at the kitchen counter, steaming mugs of coffee in their hands.

"*You* haven't seen Troy, have you?" Jela asked Sumner once noticing her. The question was spoken like an accusation, as though she and Troy were playing a cruel joke on her.

"Not since yesterday," she answered, then, internally: *But I* heard *him arguing with you hours after I last saw him.* "What's going on?" She asked once, noticing concern marking Blane's features.

"He's not here," he said with a shrug. The gesture suggested Troy's absence wasn't a big deal, but the storm clouds of worry gathering in his eyes contradicted that aloof gesture. "He likes to go for long jogs or walks when he has a lot on his mind," he added.

"I've never known him to do that," Jela said, defense-heavy in her words.

Blane's lips slightly parted. *That's because you don't know him like I do.* Sumner could see those words forming themselves on his tongue. She could hear how harsh they would have been spoken, and the sizzle of Jela's skin as those words embedded themselves in her.

"Have you tried to call or text him?" Sumner asked. Jela cut her gaze to her, her eyes daggers, their blades searing red with anger.

"It's the first thing I did," she spat. "His phone isn't with him. It's in the room on the nightstand."

That wasn't like him, especially since his sister was expected to go into labor any day. He had been on his phone more than usual, checking in with his sister for updates. Sumner recalled Troy and Jela arguing about the time he spent on his phone during the car ride to the Airbnb.

A toothy knowledge squirmed awake in the pit of her stomach, awaken by a torrent of panic. She shunned that knowledge, however, refusing to examine it and listen to the darkness it spewed, no matter how many truths lay buoyant in its sludge.

Sumner found herself outside a few hours later. They were scheduled to go rafting, but fun was the last thing anyone wanted to have. The tension inside was thick, hostility brewing at its center, its promise for mayhem was becoming more profound the longer Troy's absence went. She couldn't bare being sucked into the negativity suspended in the house, or the horror of what could be dwelling in the basement.

Stop thinking! She hissed inward.

She sat on a bench in front of the house. The bench had a flowerbed on either side of it. The floral scent would had been welcomed and enjoyed any other time. Their scent was overwhelming, nauseating when riding a rough thrust of wind. She was rising to her feet to move away from them when her attention was stolen by a car driving into the cul-de-sac.

It was a nondescript, white car, no more than three or four years old. It was the car someone would drive if they spent their life willfully blending into the crowd. The car pulled into the driveway to the house nearest the Airbnb on its left side. A man of average height and weight slid from the vehicle. She assumed his facial features were just as unrememberable as the rest of him, but she wasn't able to tell, for he purposefully avoided eye contact. She found that to be odd, considering how the cul-de-sac's residents seem to rush to their windows whenever she and the others were out and about.

"Excuse me!" She called out, only half aware she had done so. She was hurrying through the front yard. Was the man quickening his pace? She quickened hers in return. "Excuse me, sir!" She said again, only a few feet from him.

He spun around, his simple features dressed in annoyance. "Yes?"

She spent a moment tongue-tied. She pursued the man on pure impulse, and now she had his attention, she was unsure why she sought it out in the first place. "My friend," she began once the man's annoyance grew wary, concerned. She gave a nervous laugh, which only furthered his wariness. He took a step back from her.

"My friends and I are staying at that Airbnb," she tried again, gesturing her hand in the general direction of Snow White's place, "and it seems one of us might have misplaced." She managed a smile. "You haven't by chance seen a tall guy with a deep complexion wandering about, have you? He wouldn't be hard to miss around here."

The man's eyes swept the surrounding houses. She couldn't place the emotion in his gaze. Fear might have been there, but there was a bluer emotion too; something like sadness but not as deep. Was it pity that had intertwined itself with his fear?

He shook his head, and in a clipped tone, said, "Nope. Haven't seen him." She watched him turn around and head to his front door. She was at the curb when he called out to her.

"He's gone," the man said behind the safety of his screen door, "and it would be wise if you and your friends leave now, or you'll end up gone too." The sound of his front door shutting was like the period at the end of a gloating sentence.

The curtains to the windows in the surrounding houses flickered like guttering flames.

"We're getting the fuck out of here!" Sumner hollered upon entering the house. "Pack up, quick!" She strode through the living room to the bedroom. Inside the bedroom, she tossed her suitcase on the bed and started cramming all her belongings into it. Her progress began to slow as an image found her mind's eye.

The pale arm she had glimpsed on the first night here had slender, delicate fingers, and the nails of those fingers were painted red—blood red. The same as Snow White's. She wasn't surprised by this. Hadn't she suspected it all along? *And Troy is probably dead because you refused to acknowledge this*, she scolded herself. *You put everyone in danger because you coul—*

Silence.

It lay thick in the air, suffocating and oppressive. The terror she had been outrunning since concluding her brief conversation with the man next door finally caught up to her. It pounced and mauled her. It dug its talons into her flesh, it imbued her with its venom.

"Blane!" She shirked, darting from the bedroom then

screamed once seeing a figure walking down the stairs. It was a powerful scream, one that clawed up her throat, its force causing her to nearly lose her footing.

The figure froze, just as startled as Sumner was. The pall of terror cleared from her eyes, and she registered the figure as Jela.

"You scared the hell outta me," Jela said, yanking earbuds from her ears.

"Where's Blane?" Sumner demanded.

Jela crinkled her nose. "He's with that woman." She waved her hand dismissively toward the kitchen. The swell of panic must have translated to her face, for Jela's features softened a notch when asked, "What's wrong?"

She couldn't tell her about the creature stalking through the house at nightfall and its putrid smell, that it might have stolen Troy in his slumber, or how said creature might share the same flesh as their hostess. Any sane person would deem such information as delusions from a mad woman. So, instead, Sumner presented her with the husk of the truth, its entrails scooped out, its blood drained.

"Troy is missing because of that woman," she said. "And now Blane is with her. I need you to call the police. I'm going to go downstairs." Her last sentence came without thought or warning, but when those words left her lips, she knew them to be true.

Jela's eyes widened, became alive, yet not by Sumner's fear but with the prospect of drama. Then that spark dimmed a fraction. "I can't call anyone. The reception went out," she said, shaking the phone she held as if it were proof. "That's why Blane is with that woman, he's helping her fix it."

Sumner's panic deepened. It was the perfect ruse. "Go outside to call the police," she said, "and stay there until they show up. Don't come back in." She hurried to the basement door, not waiting for Jela's response. She hesitated just a second before letting herself through.

She stood on a landing, staring down the basement's dark

throat. The odor was the strongest yet. It reached up to her from the house's bowels and assaulted her with vehement hatred, clinging to her clothing, bleeding into her skin. Whimpering penetrated through her haze of fear. It was soft, barely audible, but unmistakable, and she recognized its owner.

"Blane," she whispered, descending the stairs at an ungraceful gait, the darkness chilling her the deeper she journeyed. It was reckless to move with such haste, without thought or preamble, she knew this but lost all care at that sad, pitiful sound emitting from her brother. At the bottom of the stairs was a short hallway with an open door to a small bathroom to her right. Warily, she turned left at the end of the hallway and gasped.

Before her was a room, the walls, ceiling and floor covered in perhaps millions of gleaming threads of white silk layered upon each other. No, not silk, she realized when stepping onto it. It was sticky beneath her feet but not wet and thick like glue.

She bent to examine it, but the action aborted at a muffled protest coming from above. She glanced up, and saw, half submerged in the sticky, gossamer matter, Blane. He was shaking his head, just barely, his eyes wide with fright, his mouth covered in the glistening gossamer. Beside him was a body wrapped from head to toe in the gossamer like a mummy. *Troy*.

"I prefer men," a familiar voice said, "they have more of a full-bodied taste, if you will. Women are sweeter. I'll dabble, but only when necessary."

Shadows peeled away from Snow White's nude body. Her breasts, torso and thighs were covered in a thin veil of coarse hair. And limbs were jutting from her back, four on each side, at least five feet in length, coated in thick, dark hair. They weren't human, not in the slightest; they were all bent at the femorotibial joint, like an insect. No, not just any insect. A spider.

Snow White smiled, flashing a mouthful of sharp teeth. "But a woman's sweetness turns bitter when afraid. It's best to let them marinate in their fear."

Sumner turned and ran, terror too strong of an emotion to keep her frozen by it. She hadn't even made it to the stairs when her feet became bound at the ankles. She fell to the ground, her body too slow to respond. Her pain was a visual of bursting stars when her head knocked against the floor. The collision weakened her, her fight dissipating like coiling smoke.

She could see Snow White through blurry vision. Her jaw was unhinged like a snake's, spewing glistening, white ribbons. Those ribbons were what bound her feet together. They moved up her body, securing her in a terrible cocoon, the warmth of the ribbons was oddly comforting.

Dragging footsteps sounded above, and then the next-door neighbor spoke in a strained voice: "I got the other girl, had to knock her out. Feisty little wench, she was."

"Bring her down," Snow White said. "Have the others get rid of the car. Make it look like an accident."

"The police might start gettin' suspicious. You can't have too many of your occupants disappearing."

Snow White stood at Sumner's side and smiled down at her, her beauty blighted by maleficence. "Don't you worry," she said, "I wear the perfect disguise."

Mercy Brown,
ARE YOU A VAMPIRE?

STEPHANIE RABIG

M y eyes open.

Not my real eyes, of course—those decayed long ago—but whatever passes for my eyes in the spirit world.

I don't wake up of my own volition. Someone is knocking on my grave again, asking the question.

Mercy Brown, are you a vampire?

They giggle as they ask it. Once upon a time, I didn't blame them for that; I even looked upon them with fondness. Silly games, the type my siblings and I had played when we were young.

But after over a century...

I just want to rest.

They won't let me rest.

———

"Shh! I think I heard something!"

"Oh, come on. No you didn't. This is just some stupid Bloody Mary rip-off; it's not going to work."

"No way. Mercy Brown came first."

"She may have *died* first, but I bet the legend is—"

"Did you hear that?"

"Oh my god, Jane," Aubrey said, though she offset her chiding tone by giving her friend's shoulder a gentle squeeze. "It was just a raccoon or something. Calm down." She glanced away from Jane, looking to Shawn instead. "This isn't going to work. Can we go home now?"

"Come on! Give it a minute, huh? Billie said when she did this, she saw Mercy floating over her tombstone!"

"Billie was probably high," Aubrey said.

"When is Billie not high?" Jane added.

"Hey, shut up! That's my sister."

"Your stoner sister," Delaney teased.

"Look, you didn't see her face when she came back in from the cemetery. She was terrified."

"So why are we doing this, then?"

"Don't be a chickenshit, Jane."

"I'm not a chickenshit," Jane huffed, crossing her arms. "There's just a million other things we could be doing right now."

"Each of us picks something to do on Halloween. Them's the rules. Just so happens my boyfriend has weird taste in entertainment," Delaney said, leaning over to give Shawn a loud kiss on the cheek. Shawn laughed and made a show out of pushing him away.

"At least this is different! You'd really rather be home watching Friday the 13th for the millionth time?"

"Yes," Jane and Aubrey echoed, and Shawn groaned.

"Okay, fine," he said. "Nothing's happening anyway."

Jane started to turn away, and Shawn knocked hard on the tombstone. "Hey, Mercy! You in there? You're kind of embarrassing me right now."

Aubrey laughed. "Give it up, Shawn."

"Never. Mercyyyyyyyy," he moaned, holding his phone underneath his chin like a flashlight. "We'll just come back next yearrrrrr..."

"You're dating a dumbass," Jane laughed, and Delaney grinned and wrapped an arm around Shawn's waist.

"Yeah, I know. Your turn, Aubrey. What're we doing now?"

"Well," Aubrey said, rubbing her hands together and grinning, "I've got a few dozen eggs in the trunk, and Mrs. Hudson lives about six blocks away..."

Shawn and Delaney both let out excited yells and ran toward the cemetery gates. Aubrey stared after them, smiling, and Jane touched her shoulder. "You sure?"

"Oh, absolutely. That asshole has had it coming all year."

Jane nodded. Their history teacher hated the fact that Shawn and Delaney were openly dating, and came up with excuse after excuse to send one or both of them to the principal. After claiming that they'd stolen her lesson plans and vandalized her desk, she'd even managed to get them suspended from school for two days.

"What if we get caught?" Jane asked.

"We won't. I've got masks, and I've been keeping an eye on her house for the past couple of weeks. All her lights are out by 8:oo; she's dead to the world by now. Besides, Shawn and Del aren't the only ones she's been shit to. I wouldn't be surprised if we get there to egg the place and there's a line around the block."

———

I followed them. I floated into the car after them, sitting on the driver's side in the back, still content to be unseen.

The streets had changed again. I vaguely remembered the first time I'd seen a car...the sudden noise and fast motion had frightened me so badly I'd fled back to my grave, missing my opportunity to make sure one of my tormentors never came back.

I'd gotten used to cars in the years since, though I could never tell exactly what they'd look like from one journey out to the next. Sometimes they were enormous, and other times they looked like my gravestone would weigh more. People changed, too, at least in terms of the clothes they wore and the accessories they carried. *They* never changed enough, never gained the sense and compassion to just leave me alone.

These four laughed and carried on as they drove to go vandalize some poor woman's house. I thought about murdering them before they could get the chance, but once the ones who had touched my grave were dead, my connection to the living world was gone, and I would be trapped in the gray again, unable to do anything but wait for the next person who asked the question.

Mercy Brown, are you a vampire?

What a ridiculous notion.

I can't blame my father for being temporarily taken with it—I knew, as my spirit awoke to them slicing open my body, that they could not have done so without his permission—but he was terrified. He had lost Mother, Mary Olive, and me, and was so very close to losing Edwin as well. Allowing my heart and liver to be burned and turned into a tonic for Edwin was awful, but I would have forgiven him far worse. He was only trying to save his child. That kind of fear can turn the most God-fearing of men into a monster.

What fear did these chattering pranksters have? Some pretended to be frightened as they and their friends disturbed my grave, but it was a laughing, shrieking false fear. The kind I'd once experienced when Edwin would jump out at me as I came in from finishing my chores. There was no threat behind that fear.

At least, not that they believed in yet.

It's selfish of me, but I do wish they'd cut open Mary Olive or even Mother as well. Then, perhaps, I could have some company to while away the years. Mother had been a calm heart in our home, steadying us all through an honest calamity or the smaller indignities of sibling quarrels. And Mary Olive had been quick to see the humor in any situation; she might well have been able to coax me into laughing along with the living.

But no one is here. My entire family escaped into death and none of them—not even Edwin, for whom my body suffered so many indignities—has visited me.

I know they're unable. Unlike me, their bodies were buried whole and untouched. But in my darker moments, I wonder if they're unwilling. If they've seen what my existence is now, and don't want to risk being cursed in a similar manner by showing themselves to me.

———

"That was amazing," Delaney said, pulling off the clown mask Aubrey had bought for him. "We should do that every year. Maybe every six months? Halloween in April; she'll never expect it."

Aubrey laughed and drove away from Mrs. Hudson's house. "My only regret is that the eggs weren't rotten."

"There's always next time," Shawn said, kissing the top of Delaney's head as they cuddled together in the backseat. "Thanks, Aubrey."

"Anytime. Jane, you're the last one of the night," she said. "We stayed 20 minutes each alone in the old Curtis place; knocked on Mercy Brown's grave; egged a jerk's house...what's our finale?"

"Would you guys think I was a wuss if I just wanted to watch a movie?"

"Of course!" Shawn said, leaning forward to ruffle her hair. "But you're *our* wuss."

"What do you want to watch?" Aubrey asked.

"We could go classic," Jane said. "Do a Stephen King marathon? But not ones like IT or The Shining, some of the ones we haven't seen in forever. Christine, Maximum Overdrive..."

"Oh man, Maximum Overdrive!" Delaney exclaimed. "That is the cheesiest goddamn movie in the world and I love it." He laughed, pitching his voice into a falsetto. "Currrrr-*tis*, are you dead?!"

"My house for it, though," Shawn said. "We've got the biggest TV."

———

They pulled up in front of a house that would've held at least a dozen of mine and piled out of the car. I floated behind them, listening as they talked about what movies they were going to watch and whose turn it was to gather snacks.

The first few times I was summoned, I didn't really mind. I didn't hurt anyone. I followed the ones who'd knocked back to their homes and just watched. They were fascinating to me then, the still-living, and I enjoyed the opportunity to see what life was like now. Everyone who knocked was my age or younger, and I saw myself in them.

Now I wandered the house, looking at pictures and bedrooms and trophies, all the odd accouterments of life, and I wondered which of the possessions in Shawn's bedroom his family would bury with him.

There was one other room in the house that wasn't empty. There was a young woman there, sitting in the dark at her open bedroom window, idly smoking a cigarette. I turned, letting her be. She could either find the bodies in the morning or see part of it happen.

It took some time, but I waited until one of them split off from the group.

I hadn't been alone when I died, and while I knew my family meant to be comforting, there's something especially horrid about endlessly coughing, unable to catch your breath, unable to get any air, and seeing the hopelessness in your loved ones' eyes. Knowing that they're right there, right beside you, and yet unable to do a thing to save your life.

If I can, I kill my tormentors when they're alone.

But I don't wait hours upon hours, not anymore. I don't have much kindness left, and what I do have, I won't squander.

Jane excuses herself and heads down the hall to a bathroom.

She doesn't reach her destination.

I only gave her time for her eyes to widen in fear, time to draw in part of a breath to scream, and then I snapped her neck. A quick death. No lingering for months or even years.

Kindness.

———

"Anyone else want pizza?"

"Oooh. Anything that keeps me from cooking," Aubrey said. "What toppings?"

"Pepperoni!" Delaney said.

"Jane's been on a hot wings kick lately," Shawn said. "Think she'll want those?"

"Probably," Aubrey said. "I'll go ask. And I'll see if your sister wants anything."

She got up and left the room, freezing when she turned the corner in the hall and saw Jane sprawled on the floor.

"Holy shit, hon, you only had three glasses of wine," she said, forcing humor into her voice because if she stayed calm, if she didn't panic, then this wouldn't be a situation they'd need to panic *about*. Jane wasn't the best at holding her liquor, and none of them had eaten a whole lot today, that was all, that had to be all...

Then she moved closer. Saw her friend's face, her staring eyes.

Aubrey screamed.

———

I watched the two boys barrel out of the TV room to where Aubrey was standing, her hands fluttering down at the corpse like it was a bug she wanted to be shooed out of the house.

"She's...she's..." Aubrey stammered, and I popped into view above Jane's body, baring my teeth in a snarl.

I didn't used to be so theatrical. Somewhere along the way, just killing them for waking me stopped being enough; I wanted them to be *scared*.

Aubrey screamed and covered her face with her hands; Shawn jumped back too quickly and tangled his feet together, crashing into the wall; Delaney just stared at me, his mouth opening and closing in wordless terror.

Shawn recovered and scrambled back to his feet, pushing Aubrey behind him and then grabbing Delaney's shoulders, turning him away from me.

The three of them huddled together, reminding me of the gossiping villagers back when I was alive. "Did you hear about Mary Olive?" they'd say. "Such a shame. Hasn't even been three years since poor George lost his wife..."

They talked then, and this group talked now, endless chatter, none of it meaning a thing. Just noise.

Then I realized exactly what Shawn was saying.

"It's going to be okay," he whispered, herding both of them back toward the TV room. "I promise. I'm not going to let anything happen to you."

How dare he use those words? I thought. How dare he make the same promises my father had made to my mother, to my sister, to *me*, when he knew the truth the whole time?

Those words were worthless, he had to know that, everyone knew that, why did they keep *saying* them?

Worthless, I screamed, or tried to, all that came out was a furious hiss as I wrapped my hands around Delaney's throat, my talons digging through the skin and into the soft tissue and blood beneath.

Shawn let out a howl and tried to push me away but it was too late, I could see the knowledge in his eyes and feel it flowing across my hands, a seemingly endless cascade of blood.

It was Shawn's turn to freeze, just staring at me, and Aubrey's turn to try and take charge, pulling him back. It was interesting, to see how people behaved in a sudden emergency, see how their roles shifted and changed once they were pushed to and then past their breaking point.

Shawn followed after his friend like a sobbing child, and they raced up the stairs to the room I'd discovered was occupied earlier.

"Billie!" Shawn cried as Aubrey turned on the light. "Billie, it's Del. She...oh god, she..."

"Mercy Brown killed Delaney and Jane!" Aubrey exclaimed, and the young woman in the window put out her cigarette, hurrying to her brother.

Seeing her in full light instead of the shadows of her room...I knew her.

She was now a little older than I'd been when I'd died, but I remembered her as a gap-toothed child, all alone, staring up at me in absolute terror as I hovered above the stone she'd just tapped on.

"Oh my god oh my god it's you I'm so sorry, please don't eat me or tear out my heart I'm really sorry I didn't know you were real!" she'd babbled, unable to take her eyes off me.

And I'd spared her.

By the time the memory loosed its hold on me, she was gone, as was her brother and their friend.

It didn't matter. They had called me, and I would answer.

———

"We are not going to—"

"Yes, we are! I'm going to fix this. God, Shawn, how could you do this? Why the hell would you knock on her grave, I told you what—"

"I'm sorry," he sobbed. "I'm sorry."

"Shit," Billie murmured, pausing in their headlong run toward the cemetery to pull her brother into her arms. "No, I'm sorry. You must've thought I was playing a prank on you."

"Del...and Jane, she was..."

"I know, kiddo."

"Guys," Aubrey said, looking around nervously. "Come on. We need to go."

Billie nodded, grabbing hold of Shawn's hand and pulling him after her for a few steps when he started to sink to the ground instead.

"Are you sure about the cemetery?" Aubrey asked.

"I saw her once. She let me go. I'm going to talk to her again. She's not a boogeyman or something; she's a human being. She'll listen."

She has to, Billie thought. She knew she'd been given a miracle that night ten years ago; she just needed one more. For Shawn's sake.

Aubrey was ahead of them, unencumbered by a traumatized Shawn, and as she turned toward the entrance to the cemetery, she was suddenly whipped into the bushes in front of the Kellerman's old house, letting out a horrifying, pained wail.

"Aubrey!" Shawn screamed.

Billie let go of his hand long enough to try and help, but one look at Aubrey told her it was too late. She'd been torn open, throat to belly.

"It was my idea," Shawn cried, as Billie tried to block his view of her body, tried to usher him to the cemetery. "It was my idea to knock, she should be after me, just me..."

"Enough," Billie said. "She's not—she's not going to get you. Come on. Over the fence. Come on!" she yelled when he just stood there.

He finally moved, and once she was also over the fence she grabbed his hand again, dragging him toward a grave she'd never intended to visit again, but the location of which she remembered all too well.

She rapped hard on the stone, looking around frantically— she hadn't seen Mercy at all when she'd taken Aubrey, and somehow that was a million times worse—and then remembered.

"Mercy Brown," she yelled. "Are you a vampire?"

She nearly lost her will, nearly collapsed in a heap just like her brother, when Mercy appeared over her tombstone, eyes blazing with an inhuman fury and her ribcage cracked open and split apart, exposing where her heart had once been.

"Wait, please," Billie said, her throat trying to close around the words. "Please. He's just a kid. He's seventeen. He didn't mean it. It's...it's my fault. I told him about seeing you, and I thought it'd scare him off, but he thought I was just making it up. I didn't convince him. And that's my fault. Okay? Please leave him alone."

———

I stared down at her, recognizing the desperation in her voice, the fierce love she felt for her brother, the same as I'd felt for Edwin.

I began to fade. I would spare him. Would spare her, as I had done once before.

Once before.

And what had she done? Had she respected that gift, kept her mouth shut so others would leave me alone?

No. She'd told.

The young woman's face faded, replaced by so, so many others, the ones who made it impossible for me to see my own family again, the ones who keep me trapped in this limbo.

Almost before I realized what I was doing, I'd torn off her face. She collapsed, landing next to her brother, who screamed at the sight of her.

He didn't scream for long.

I used to feel gratitude when I felt myself fading when I returned to the gray, but now there was only exhaustion and anger and wondering when I'd be called forward yet again.

I stared at the two bodies in front of my grave, their blood seeping into the ground, and for a few seconds felt regret at the choice I'd made.

It faded quickly.

They didn't matter. Just two more in a long line.

My name is Mercy Brown. I was a 19-year-old girl who happened to get sick.

I wasn't a vampire then, and am not a vampire now.

After so long down here, denied any peace in what should be my final resting place...

I am something so much worse.

it wasn't a
SQUONK

JUDITH SONNET

"You have to believe me!" Branson exclaimed. "It was a Squonk! I know it!" The poor boy was close to tears. He had been arguing all day that he had seen a mysterious creature rootling around in the woods beside their camp.

"There's no such thing." Dean rolled his eyes and kicked the gravel. "It's made up. Just like everything in that silly book."

Branson lowered his head toward the tome sitting on his scrawny legs. Branson carried his book of mythological creatures with him wherever he went. It was his Bible.

After witnessing the creature, he had spent much of the day looking through the weather-beaten pages of his book, seeking answers. After landing on a description of the Squonk, he had gasped aloud and woken up his bunkmates with a few hard shakes. Now, Dean, Clive, and Ronnie were all rubbing the sleep from their eyes and trying to keep their voices low enough so as not to alert the rest of the cabin to their conversation. None of the other kids would have cared, but Matheson would have pitched a fit. Their burly counselor was cool most of the time but he hated being roused from his sleep. He was lying on a cot with an arm hanging out from his sleeping bag. He was only a few feet away from Branson, and the kid was starting to hyperventilate. Dean tried to hush him but he kept insisting that "it was definitely a Squonk!"

"What the hell is a Squonk anyways?" Ronnie asked. The tallest kid in their foursome, Ronnie had rich parents and never talked to anyone from their group outside of camp. His voice was affluent and accented.

"Don't ask. We'll never shut him up!" Clive rasped. Large and freckled, Clive was often the object of ridicule at school. Camp meant solace to him. No one cared to make fun of him when he wasn't even half as nerdy or as laughable as the boys that surrounded him. A little extra weight was nothing compared to the heights of dorkiness that Branson had reached. He was like "nerd camouflage".

Branson held his book open and presented it to his pals. On one page there was a black and white ink drawing and on the other, there was a block of barely legible text. The writing was so small it was no wonder Branson needed magnifying eyeglasses.

"Have you always been such a geek?" Dean asked harshly.

"Look! This is what I saw!" Branson proclaimed.

"Shut up! You'll wake the whole camp up!"

"But look!"

Dean did. The drawing was ugly. It was of a fat and wrinkled creature that was covered in thick moles and warts. Its squashed face was covered in tears and its mouth seemed to be caught mid-tremble. It was standing on four bed-post legs, and its feet were clubbed. It looked like a pug mixed with a warthog.

"Yuck." Dean took the book out of Branson's hand and got a closer look at the picture. "That's fuckin' ugly."

Dean was a stout boy with thick eyes, a crew cut, and an array of pimples. He was the eldest boy in the cabin —apart from their snoozing counselor. He had taken on the mantle of leadership for their gang, simply due to his seniority.

The boys were all in middle school. Before long, they'd be too old for Camp Whippoorwill... and this imminent conclusion loomed over them like a guillotine's blade. Ronnie barely spoke to them outside of camp as it was. Dean was going to join the football team and would be carried away from Clive and Branson. And Branson was just too weird to be much of a companion. Dean knew he'd miss the good times he shared with these kids... but he also knew that they would hold him back if he remained in their company. Dean wanted to make friends with fellow jocks. He wanted a girlfriend too. He didn't have the patience to sit around and listen to Branson describe mythical creatures anymore.

Dean handed the book back to Branson and said: "Yeah. Gross. Go back to sleep Branson."

"Listen to this though!" Branson turned his book around and

began to read from the thin script.

"'The Squonk is a creature of folklore that originated from the lumberyards of Northern Pennsylvania'! You know what camp Whippoorwill used to be back in the day? It was a lumberyard!"

"So?" Ronnie asked and swept a lock of brown hair away from his dewy eyes.

"Keep listening… 'the Squonk is said to be so ugly it only comes out on moonless nights so as not to risk seeing its reflection in the surface of the rivers and streams it lives by'. I saw it right by the river while we were canoeing!"

"You didn't see a magic monster, Branson." Dean insisted. "You saw a wild boar or… or a deer… or something. You almost flipped our canoe too. You need to stop freaking out every time you get excited about somethin—"

"'If one wants to find a Squonk, all one must do is follow its tears. Aware of how hideous it looks, the Squonk is always weeping'!" Branson snapped his book closed. "I know exactly where it was, you guys! We can go there and then follow its tears to it! And then we'll be famous for proving it's real!"

"I don't want to go snipe hunting," Dean said.

"Squonk hunting," Ronnie corrected.

"My brother says Snipes are actually a real type of bird," Clive added.

"Your brother would." Dean sneered.

"You guys!" Branson whined, making no effort to lower his voice. "I can prove it's real! C'mon!"

"What are we supposed to do, huh? Sneak out? If you really care that much… we'll look for it tomorrow." Dean said.

Branson mumbled and adjusted his massive spectacles. "I just… you think I'm faking but I'm not! I saw it and it looked just like this!"

He thrust the book toward Dean.

"I saw its face sticking out of the bushes and it was all squished and covered in moles and warts and—"

"We'll look tomorrow. If you want." Dean tossed the book back and climbed into his bunk. "Just… go to sleep, dude."

Ronnie and Clive retreated as well, following the leader. Branson stayed up, reading his book by flashlight and muttering to himself. "It had to be a Squonk. It couldn't be anything else…"

"Shut up, kid!" A random cabin-mate squawked.

Dean fell asleep as Branson's voice finally trailed away into a whisper like a stream reaching its end.

The next day, the four boys rushed into the mess hall for breakfast. The sun was heavy above them and Dean was squinting as he chewed on a stale piece of French toast. He had forgotten all about Branson's stories, but his reprieve was short-lived.

"So, do you guys want to go find the Squonk today?" Branson asked as a strand of syrup dripped out of his mouth.

"God." Dean sighed and inhaled his paper cup of orange juice. "It's not real… nerd." He felt like a bully saying it, but Branson was really acting up.

"We can look around." Ronnie cut in. "I didn't want to stick around the cabins during free time anyways."

"We're not going into the woods and searching for something that ain't real." Dean scoffed.

"I'm down, Branson," Clive said as he licked his sticky fingers. "C'mon, Dean. What can it hurt?"

"We'll get ticks," Dean said. "We'll get ticks and we'll all look like idiots. And when we come out of the woods and people ask what we were looking for we'll have to lie."

"Branson said he saw it," Clive said with a shrug.

"He saw a shadow and his mind filled in the blanks!" Dean almost shouted. "He's just leading us on a goose chase!"

"You don't have to come with us," Branson interjected.

"Of course, I'm coming with you." Dean shoveled another piece of French toast into his mouth and spoke around it. "If I didn't come along then you'd all get lost…"

After eating and throwing their paper trays into the trash, the boys left the mess hall in one group. After breakfast, the kids were allowed to run around and play freely. A few girls were by the river, skipping stones. Another group of children were running toward the swing seats, pushing each other as they went. A unit of counselors sat on the porch of Cabin B. They were talking amongst themselves, and none of them saw the boys as they walked into the woods together.

———

"It was around here where I saw him," Branson said with dramatic pomp. "He was poking his head out from the crotch of that tree, just watching us as we paddled by."

He's laying it on thick. Dean pocketed his hands and kicked a jagged rock into the nearby water. It plunked beneath the surface and vanished from sight.

"What did he look like again?" Ronnie asked. Dean could tell their affluent friend was trying to be charitable to Branson. His patience was short and before long, Ronnie and Dean would be in the same exasperated camp.

"He was just like the picture in the book! His face was all smashed and warty, and his eyes were so small and black! They looked like pieces of coal!"

"Pieces of shit," Dean muttered.

"I just saw his face, but when he vanished, I'm sure he was on all fours," Branson stated, ignoring Dean's jest. He pulled his book up and flipped back to the page about the Squonk. It was dog-eared. "It says that you can find a Squonk by following its teardrops! Everyone start looking around the ground by the tree here!" Branson was becoming quite the ringleader.

Dean kicked up some dirt and leaves, pretending he was looking as earnestly as his pals were. Ronnie was doing a good job acting but Clive —bless his heart—seemed genuinely invested. He rifled through ferns and peered beneath roots, looking for the elusive tears.

"Here it is guys! This'll lead us right to him!" Branson declared.

He was standing just behind the tree and toward a gentle creek. The stream was weaving through the underbrush and slipping into the river beside them.

"That's just some runoff. Those aren't fairy tears." Dean said.

"It's our Squonk's tears, all right! Why else would it be right here?"

Branson beamed with delight as if he had somehow won a debate with some form of tact. Dean raised a brow and scowled.

How many wedgies does this kid get when I'm not around? Dean thought with a snort.

"Well, let's follow the trail! He can't be far! These tears are fresh!" Branson dashed along the side of the stream, ushering his friends along. They followed close by, barely keeping pace with the energetic dork.

"What do we do with a Squonk when we find it?" Clive asked. "Can we make a wish?"

"What would you wish for?" Ronnie asked.

"A million dollars."

"And what would you spend it on?"

"I dunno," Clive shucked his shoulders. "Anything I want?"

"A million dollars won't get you very far anymore. Why not ask for a billion?" Dean said as he stumbled over a knotted thatch of exposed roots.

"I mean, yeah. Why not? How about it, Branson? Will the Squonk give me a million dollars?"

"I dunno." Branson said. All of his confidence drained away. "The book didn't say anything about wishes. But maybe that's because no one's ever gotten close enough to try!"

"Does anyone have a camera?" Ronnie asked. "We'd need pictures of the Squonk... if we find it."

"I wanna take it back to camp!" Branson said. "Who needs photos when you can show off the real thing?"

"Will you take it for walks and make sure it has food and water?" Dean spoke up, imitating a stern adult.

"I don't know what Squonks eat!" Branson laughed.

Jovial and determined, the boys pushed through the forest. The trees grew tight around them, hugging the sides of the thin creek. The water burbled listlessly, never growing deeper than an ankle, or thicker than a plank. If they hadn't been looking, Dean was sure they wouldn't have even taken note of this pathetic stream.

What if Branson is right and you guys actually find some kind of mythical creature? Dean thought. *I mean, he obviously isn't... but what if?*

Ronnie's digital watch began to chirp. He held it up and looked at the time. "*Drat.* Free time is ending soon. We have to go back." He said.

"No, we don't!" Branson insisted. "We haven't even seen the Squonk yet!"

"No," Dean said and stopped walking. "Ronnie's right. Matheson will send a search party after us if we're not there for Arts and Crafts—"

Branson whirled around. "Screw Arts and Crafts! When we come back with the Squonk, they won't care that we were tardy!"

"Hey!" Clive spoke up. "Calm down, buddy. It's just a game. We can come back and play Squonk-hunt later—"

Branson turned around and continued down the stream, ignoring his friends.

"Branson! Come on!" Dean shouted as his buddy vanished through the thickets. "Branson! It's just make-believe! There's no such thing as a Squonk!"

But it was too late. Branson was already gone, determined to find something that didn't exist. Dean sighed and kicked the water.

"What do we do?" Clive asked.

"You and Ronnie head back. I'm going to chase after the little twerp. Tell Matheson he's sick and I'm taking care of him. Or something." Dean said and trudged forward.

"You sure?" Ronnie asked.

"No. But I'm not going to let him get lost. Just cover for us, yeah?" Dean shouted over his shoulder before nudging his way around a crowd of bushes.

———

After Dean was gone, Ronnie sighed and turned toward Clive. "I guess we just head back then."

"Guess so, yeah..." Clive bowed his head.

The two boys awkwardly started to follow the stream back the way they had come. They were soundless as they went, unsure what to say to one another. Usually, Dean was the leader. Ronnie only hung out with the losers because they doted on his privileged life. Clive hung out with them because they accepted him and didn't take cheap shots at his weight. The two weren't really friends... but they were social survivalists.

Overhead, thunder boomed. Ronnie looked up toward the sky. A fat droplet of rain weaseled through the packed leaves and landed on his nose. He sneezed and wiped his face with the heel of his hand.

"Did you know it was going to rain today?" Clive asked as more drops of water pattered through the trees. The stream was going to turn into a gushing creek in a matter of moments.

"No. I didn't." Ronnie muttered.

"God. I hope they turn around. What if they get lost?" Clive said and looked back toward the direction Branson and Dean had gone.

"They'll be fine. It's just a little—" Ronnie didn't notice the sturdy shape leaping out from behind the trees until it was too late. An axe swung through the air and collided with Ronnie's chest. The air was knocked out of his lungs before his shirt and then his flesh was split open. He felt the axes head clang against his ribcage, shattering several bones in successive bursts.

Ronnie stumbled back, accidentally expunging the weapon from its meaty bed. An airy hiss followed the vacancy, as well as two quick spurts of blood that reminded Ronnie of piss streams.

The rain began to come down heavily. If Ronnie's eyes weren't already blurred with pain... he would have been blinded by the elements.

"Help!" Ronnie weakly exclaimed.

"Ronnie? Are you okay?" Clive asked.

The axe swished through the air and clipped Ronnie in the throat. Sharpened to a shimmery point, the axe didn't struggle to tear into Ronnie's sensitive flesh. Blood flew out beneath his chin and coated the front of Ronnie's assailant. It also turned upwards and flew against Ronnie's face, as if he was standing by a busted water fountain. His vital syrup filled his mouth and coated the inner walls of his nostrils.

"Help!" Ronnie gurgled before the axe hit him for the third and final time. This strike hit Ronnie directly in the chin. It was a hard uppercut that split his lower jaw in half. He could feel his teeth popping out of place and tumbling down his front and into his throat. As he gasped for breath, he could feel a stray tooth wiggle out of the hole that had been seared into his esophagus. The tooth hit the ground a fraction of a second after Ronnie had died. He followed it, his body smashing into the quickly moistening earth. With a wet rasp and a low belch, Ronnie was officially beyond saving.

Clive stood by, frozen with fear. He had wet his pants as his friend was brutally murdered. The flurry of blood and broken skin distracted him, and so he didn't take in the appearance of Ronnie's murderer... until it was too late. The shadowy killer juked sideways and then forward, skirting Ronnie's corpse and making a beeline toward Clive.

"Wait, wait... *wait!*" Clive held up his hands in defense.

The killer swung his sharpened axe. It razed Clive's palms open. Blood seeped between his knuckles and iced his wrists.

Clive yipped and stumbled backward. He released a high-pitched squeal. It was a noise he hadn't thought himself capable of before.

The assailant drew the axe back like a baseball bat and swung toward Clive's generous belly. Clive slipped backward, dodging the axe and landing on his rump. He began to scuttle in reverse, his wounded hands digging up dirt and mud as he went. Clive breathed heavily, trying to comprehend his attacker even as he tried to evade them.

The killer followed, swinging the axe by his side.

Clive realized that the killer was weeping. Tears raced down his pudgy face and dotted the ground, vanishing amidst the raindrops.

"I don't want to die!" Clive proclaimed.

The killer said nothing. Instead, he knocked Clive in the brow with the butt of his weapon. Clive heard his skin crack open and felt a thread of blood spool down his face. He flopped onto his back and gasped like a panicked fish.

The killer began to chop into Clive like he was firewood. The axe dug red trenches across Clive's chest before lopping off his head.

Still weeping, the killer kicked the head as hard as he could. It smacked against the base of a tree, smattering the ground with fleshy strands of tissue and pink brains.

———

The rain was coming down heavily. Dean hoped that the other boys had gotten to camp by now and that they were sending a search party out for him and Branson.

"C'mon, Branson!" Dean shouted, pushing through the branches. The smaller kid was rushing ahead, barreling along the path of the steadily widening stream in search of his mystical beast. "You have to slow down, buddy! I can't keep up!"

Branson ignored him and pressed onward. Dean couldn't help but admire his passion, even if it was misguided.

"Why are you doing this?" Dean shouted.

"Because I want to prove everyone wrong!" Branson returned.

Dean huffed. "You aren't proving anything! You're just being a little *shit*!"

"I thought you were different! I thought you all cared! But you're just like the kids at school! You don't believe me and you never will... unless I prove it!" Branson paused. "I saw it, Dean! I really did see a Squonk and it's *real* and I'll *show* you!" He was crying.

Dean felt bad for Branson. He should have been kinder and gentler to him. Dean realized that he was as much to blame for this situation as Branson was.

"I'm sorry, dude," Dean said. "I shouldn't have... I should've been... I mean... I'm just sorry."

Branson stumbled on the sloping ground. He almost tipped into the creek. Dean rushed up to his side and held him steady.

"I'm sorry," Dean said.

Branson wiped his tears away and sniffled.

"We're going to catch a cold, you know?" Dean laughed.

"Huh. Yeah," Branson moaned.

"Hey. Let's head back. We'll get yelled at by Matheson but I'm sure he'll be happy we didn't get in any serious trouble. Wanna get some blankets and read some comics by the space heater?"

"S-sure." Branson's teeth chattered.

Dean wrapped an arm around the smaller boy and began to drag him back the way they came.

And then, they heard it.

Up ahead, Dean and Branson both heard something moan pitifully.

When Dean had been in kindergarten, his dad took him hunting. Dean hadn't comprehended what the sport entailed until it was too late and his father had shot a buck through its back. Dean would never forget its low cries.

That was exactly what *this* sounded like. It was like a wounded animal weeping as it died.

"Shit." Dean hissed and began to backpedal.

"Wait!" Branson froze in place. "Is it..."

The thing that trudged out of the woods didn't look human.

Its face was coated in warts, fatty pockets, and infected boils. Pus and gruesome juices oozed out of its craggy face. Its eyes were beady and soaked in tears. Its lower face was a bag of bunched-up wrinkles. Its mouth looked like a closed fist.

It was wearing a yellow rain jacket and a pair of stained jeans. Its naked belly was furry and covered in sores and scratches. It smelled like roadkill and sickness.

It dragged an axe beside it.

Dean shrieked with fright, but Branson bravely stepped forward. "Look, Dean! It's just as I described it!" He pulled his book out from the back of his pants and flipped to the dog-eared page. "It's a Squonk!"

The killer hefted his axe up and swept it through the air and toward Branson. Dean acted on instinct, shoving his friend aside. The axe clipped the side of Dean's head, removing a sticky chunk of his scalp. Blood fumed out of the wound and coated Dean's face. He tipped sideways and collapsed against the ground.

Branson gasped and stepped backward. The book was becoming soggy in his hands as the rain fell into its open pages.

"Uhhhh." Dean moaned as if he was reacting to a bad head cold.

The killer dropped down by Dean's side and flipped him over so his face was smooshed into the sodden earth. The killer reached into his side and drew a knife from his belt loop. It was a gleaming hunting knife with a wooden handle.

Without hesitating, he made his first brutal puncture. He punched the blade into Dean's back, just below his shoulder blade.

Dean began to whine as the killer repeated the motion. He stabbed Dean in rapid bursts, hitting the blade up and down Dean's back. He could feel his blood cascading down his sides and filling the muddy creases in the earth beside his broken and busted body.

Dean didn't realize what the killer was doing until he had set the knife aside. The killer breathed in heavily as if he was a surgeon and he was preparing for a delicate operation. He pushed his stubby fingers into the wounds that crawled up either side of Dean's spine.

No, no, no, no, no, no, no, no, God no! Dean thought as the killer cried out in misery as he secured his fingers around the column of bone that controlled Dean's movements.

The killer dragged the spine up from Dean's back. The flesh tore apart with a sound like fabric being ripped down the middle. The spine wriggled freely, like a ridged caterpillar. Its tail bumped back and forth in the killer's greasy grasp.

Dean made a few hiccup sounds as his arms and legs went numb.

I'm dying. He realized. *I'm just a kid but... I'm dying—*

The killer yanked on the cord like it was attached to a boat engine. The motion separated the spine from its place at the base of Dean's skull. His thoughts instantly went black and his last breath was an agitated gasp.

———

The killer dropped the white spinal cord and breathed in deeply as if he was sniffing a pungent flower. Despite his violence —or maybe because of it—he hadn't stopped weeping. Fresh tears sprang from his tiny eyes and filled in the cracks left by his itchy boils and scars. He began to stomp on Dean's corpse, smooshing it into the mud and producing splashes of crimson along the legs of his already soiled jeans. After a second of emotional blindness, he remembered the other kid.

He turned around and was surprised to see that Branson was still standing in place. He had helplessly watched as his best friend was brutalized.

His book of mythological creatures remained open. The rain had washed out the pages. All that remained were black blurs of runny ink and wet papers which threatened to drip away like the petals of an overfed flower.

The killer grabbed his axe and hefted it up over his shoulder. Wiping his tears with the cuff of his rain jacket, he strode toward Branson.

Branson's lips trembled. He spoke as the killer neared him.

"I know what you are!' He said with confidence.

The killer stood still, appraising the child.

"You're... a Squonk!"

The killer cocked his head to the side, confused by the declaration.

"Y-you... you're a Squonk! A creature that's so ugly, he can't stop crying! The-they wrote about you in-n my favorite book." Branson held out the mushy tome. "T-they... my friends... they said you aren't r-real but... b-but I saw you. I knew. I never doubted it-t."

The killer stepped toward Branson, gripping the wooden handle of his axe.

"I'm right, aren't I? You're a Squonk, right?"

"Sure, Kid." The Squonk said. "Whatever you say."

Before his brains were split in two, the last thought that raced through Branson's head was this:

I knew it! I knew it! Wait until everyone at camp hears about thi—

the
LOVERS

MARKUS J WILLIAMS

Slivers of skin,
Tendon, sinew and sin—
These things you must shed
When our parts are wed.

Abattoir of tongues,
Unsheathing flesh,
You will be hung
From the crimson rungs,
Finally undressed.

I will eat you then—
Pumping muscle,
Gleaming gristle, and all—
So long as you promise me,
Until your very bones
Are picked clean,
To always let me in.

And I will leave you then—
A cemetery to be undisturbed—
In search of a new and proffering buffet,
Until my appetite is
Once more curbed.

— LOVE'S ABATTOIR

"Let me tell you a song of fantasy," he said, standing from the bed and towering over her, nude as the day he was born. The slits of moonlight that entered through the open blinds of the bedroom's single window helped only to illuminate his bare chest; all else of him was shrouded in darkness. She crawled down from the bed and onto the coarse carpet like a dog preparing to receive a treat, eager to hear her lover tell his tale.

"Yes," she said, as she scuttled on her knees towards him. "Tell me." In the pallid light of the moon, he saw her smile: pointed teeth glinting, mouth wide, sincere and hungry for his words.

"Anything that loves," he said alas, "lives." No words came further from his lips.

In the beat of silence, only the outside autumn wind could be heard in the room, howling as it went by. Realizing his song was over, she placed her hand on his breast and sighed. Her touch was warm and soft, he felt. Yet still, he winced.

"Then I'm glad to be alive," she said. "Well, as alive as this is. To live, and to love." She leaned her head forward and kissed the center of his abdomen. After removing her lips and hand, she looked up and into the darkness of his face.

"Touch me again," the darkness said back, and she complied readily.

She placed a single finger, her right index, onto his left breast —the place of his heart—and slowly began to move it gently around. The feeling of touch, though alien to him, was quite pleasant, and he decided he would watch her no more, but merely see her caress through the sensation of feeling alone. In the darkness, he closed his eyes and opened a smile, as his nerves took eyes.

Her finger ran vertically across his chest, twirling balletically as it did so, swirling slowly down. Its tip was damp, as if nervous with sweat, but showed no such sign in its traveling. He could feel the digit was curious and contemplative in its caress, debating as to where to carry itself next. At last, it found a home in the hollowed dip of his sternum and slid down. As it traveled, a blooming thread emerged from behind it, spreading red in its wake. The crimson line appeared oily in the moonlight, and was not straight, but ran crookedly along the valleys and curvature of his breastbone. There was no pain to be felt for him, however; only the warmth of her finger's tip as it glided. Finally, she reached his navel, and there she ceased her travels. She removed her finger—taking with it the comforting warmth of its tip. For a moment, all was still and bitter; the only presence that of the howling wind beyond. But then a single tear, dark in complexion, wept forth from the wound and slithered down the line. She watched in awe as it traced the trail of his chest, and down to his navel, opening the wound as it ran. Finally, it took root at the end of its journey inside the shelter of his untouched belly button. He sighed, and it slithered inside. The air entering his opened cavity was icy and crisp, yet it too did not hurt but was merely startling. Feeling venturous, he took in as deep a breath as his lungs would allow, and the two flaps of his chest opened, blooming like a flower greeting spring rain. The frigid air rushed into him, cooling his warm innards, and he smiled. Life was so sweltering, so blistering. But this—this was bliss.

"Drink from me," he finally said. The spoken words were as shocking to him as they were to her. For a moment, she hesitated, processing the words, then finally nodded in understanding. "Yes," she said and took her mouth to his wound.

He tilted himself forward, allowing the adjacent rivulets running through him to pour out of the hole. Several of the streams fell, appearing like miniature crimson waterfalls, and keeping her word, she drank from them. He again closed his eyes, as he felt his lifeblood draining from out of him. The digits of his hands were beginning to grow numb, his limbs tingly, but he cared not. All that mattered was that he must feed his beloved before him; her gluttony his only priority.

"All life consumes," he explained as his blood vacated himself, his voice filled with orgasmic agony. "Consumes lives until it too finally dies. Ah, such is life—" he looked down upon his slurping beloved, "—and death."

In the glint of moonlight, he saw her opened mouth smile again at his words, a vermillion grin of glee. The streams of blood were beginning to thin as they poured into her throat, her esophagus steadily swallowing the sustenance in rhythmic gulps. He brushed her face with his hand—yet his fingers felt nothing. They were too numb now, too drained. Nevertheless, he ran his fingers around the bottom rim of her wet lips, smearing the red stain like a butcher's lipstick. He then placed them into her opened mouth, feeling the points of her growing teeth, admiring his work.

"All life feeds," he said, still moving his senseless fingers. "And all alive things need be fed. Until, that is, when they are dead." He locked eyes with her—eyes filled with ravenous appetite; eyes of love—and then collapsed to the soaked floor. His feet, it seemed, had too grown numb to support his own weight any longer.

She gasped, but he quickly shushed her from the floor, his head twisted into the damp carpet, shrouded as ever in darkness.

"Fret not," the muffled voice came from the shadows, barely audible to her ears over the outside shrieking winds. "This is but the song of reality: for everything that lives," he said calmly, "dies. It is the cycle; to live and love and eat, then die and be eaten. We should not fight the cycle, nor should we reject the songs, but embrace them." As he spoke, she slid again on her knees across the carpet, creeping ever closer to the darkness encompassing her talking lover.

"Now drink from me, my dear," he urged as she, at last, reached him again. "Drink from my veins until the rivers of my being no longer flow. Drain me until my arteries no longer have purpose or need. Feast yourself; nourish yourself; give yourself strength and sustenance from my being, until my very mind goes. I promise you, I will live in you then—even if only for a time. But that brevity of sustenance, of life-giving, will be, to me, an eternity. Now please, my love, don't waste another drop —drink me."

With his speech said, she took him again with reluctant lips. It was a meeting of meat and mouthpiece; the flayed lips of a wounded torso, and the trembling lips of a nervous heart. She slurped once, and he sighed—one final exhale of life exiting the mortal and corrupting confines of its household. Then, with his breath gone, lost and forgotten in the stale air of the room, his body grew cold, as the warm one of hers stayed sweltering, still living and breathing and drinking.

And there she sat, silent and slurping, teeth steadily growing and sharpening, while the outside autumn wind still howled, until the sun arose extinguishing the moon and the stars, and the soft whine of commuting cars could be heard passing by beyond.

With the dawn came the rain, and with the rain fell the leaves from the dormant trees, all drifting into the billowing, autumn breeze—just as her lover had—to new and unknown lands.

Death, despite its finality, she thought, as she stood alas and moved to shut the blinds from the ever brightening world, careful as to not let the growing sunlight meet her flesh. *Death does not cause the world to end.*

No, she furthered, wiping in darkness the crusted flakes of dried blood from her lips. *It but feeds it. And after all is gone, the stars beyond will still move, and a new day will dawn, and life without you, my love, will still ignorantly carry on.*

Frostbitten petals break from their umbilical cords
of life, and drift toward the ground,
Like Prometheus loosed from his chains, finally
unbound.

The pollen-collecting bees and honey-suckling
birds return to their chore no more,
As the last remaining, reluctant leaves finally fall
to the awaiting floor.

The inevitable autumn winds begin to chant their
choir sound,
As its harmony with the reaping season is once
more found.

Rays of warmth sputter out as the cleansing
deluge begins its pour,
Greeting the reveling worms resting in our sores
—ancient inhabitants of the core.

Thus, the conquerors arise as the skies continue to
heave,
Sprouting forth from the soiled and sodden
ground to feast upon us fallen leaves.

And none will ever be left...

— THE LEAVING AND THE LEFT

all my
BASTARDS

KEN WINKLER

'll tell you why I'm soaked to the bone and shivering, friend, but first I'd like to offer you a piece of advice: Never lie with a siren.

Exotic and sweet though it may seem, I suggest you spit in your palm and think of the milkmaid instead, or the cobbler's bucktoothed daughter. If that doesn't work, then try your dear Aunt Margaret. Yes, Aunt Margaret, on her knees and scrubbing the floor, her ponderous breasts swaying like two fat infants in a cradle. Hell, you might even fancy her cat.

But never lie with a siren.

Unless...

Ah, now I have your attention. There are always exceptions, aren't there? How dull life would be if we didn't occasionally defer better sense to bitter reckoning down the road. Allow me to amend my previous warning with a caveat. Never lie with a siren, unless you find yourself stranded on a forsaken rock in the middle of an icy black sea, and have no other choice.

I had no crew, you see, as every last soul aboard The Gwendolyn Fair had been swallowed by the tides, and the ship herself had run aground, her masts toppled. The notion of doom set in, and by day three the cold had gotten into my guts and set them all aquiver. Death gaped wide like a whale's maw, eager to swallow me whole.

But then I remembered the whistle, sold to me by a destitute man at The Port of Orishen.

"It's a bad omen for a captain not to carry one," he'd urged through a set of rotted teeth while proffering a brass whistle in his filthy palm.

Talk of omens tickled the hairs in my ears. "What's this about whistles?" I asked.

"This one beckons *her*. If you find yourself in a spot of trouble, just give the whistle a blow, and she'll come to your aid. I swear it."

"Who will come to my aid?"

"The Lady of the Sea," he said, his dim eyes feigning wonder. "One crown and it's yours."

"Ludicrous!" I said, but I'd heard rumors of such whistles, the rarity of them, and wanted one, even if only to spark conversation during my next long voyage. I paid full price for the trinket and gave it no further thought, until that day on the shore.

And so, I reached into my pocket and found the whistle I had purchased from the reprobate in Orishen. A foolish hope gripped me as I approached the wide, roiling ocean. Cannon fire boomed in the darkened clouds above, portending punishment for such unholy intentions, but I ignored God's warning, put the whistle to my lips, and blew.

But the whistle made no sound.

Go ahead and laugh. I certainly did. The great Captain Jarko, disgraced by the sea, swindled by a derelict, and fated to die alone. But the whistle had, in fact, produced a frequency inaudible to human ears.

The siren emerged stark nude from the ocean at dusk, draped in kelp, with long rivulets of jet-black hair outlining the contours of a goddess. She sauntered toward me with her arms at her sides, olive skin aglow, her eyes filled with deep-sea mysteries. And I swear I'd once glimpsed this lithe creature in the deepest fathoms of slumber. But enough talk of pulchritude and dreams. Suffice it to say she owned me at first sight.

And when she pressed her breast to my parched lips, I suckled like an infant. Her briny milk revived me and roused my seafaring loins. You might think a siren's skin be cold and unpleasant to the touch, but no. The fire inside her had been stoked in Hades, and it's the Devil's truth that she writhed atop me like a serpent for hours—torturing my senses, holding me on the edge of release in a state of empty-headed bliss—until I could bear it no more. I emptied myself into her in ten excruciating spasms, down to the last seed bearing my name and likeness.

That night I awoke to her moaning in the moonlight, her

stomach bulging with life, the hands inside her stretching her flesh as though kneading dough. Then she popped, and the bastards followed—a litter of misshapen things that bore an uncanny, yet distorted resemblance to *me,* all spilling from between her legs on a filthy tide, then screeching in a multitude of tiny voices.

To say I stood aghast would be a gross understatement. She rolled her eyes toward me, and said, "You have your crew, and I have your soul." Then she sloughed off the illusion of beauty and revealed herself as the foul hag she was.

Give me a moment, as I haven't yet gained academic distance from the experience. Where was I? Oh, yes—the brood, the bargain.

I'd sired seven male pups, each one more hideous than the last, and the suckling farrow grew with a rapidity that defied all natural law. Of course, I wanted to bash in their skulls with a rock, but their mother hissed like an animal if I strayed too close.

Within a week my bastards had grown to the height of men. Muscled idiots they were, and prone to sibling violence, but they possessed enough intelligence to follow basic orders. We repaired the vessel, then set sail—the whole unholy lot of us.

Our food stores consisted of one box of lard, dried peppers, and salt. Starvation would set in before we reached civilization, but the siren devised a plan: The weakest among them would forgo their flesh and nourish the rest. She made them fight, and we subsisted on the losers, but to my dismay, this didn't decrease our ranks, as she'd taken to coupling with her children. The resulting abominations shamed the others in repulsiveness.

By the time I caught sight of land, no fewer than one hundred bastards crowded the deck, yipping and howling with excitement for the pillaging to come.

Don't judge my sin too harshly, friend. I had to kill all my bastards.

I smeared the wheelhouse in lard and set it alight while the creatures bearing my features snored in a pile around their mother below deck then dove overboard and swam ashore.

Come.

Look out the window.

There, just beyond the harbor, The Gwendolyn Fair still burns!

ABOUT THE AUTHORS

STEPHANIE ELLIS

Stephanie writes dark speculative prose and poetry and has been published in a variety of magazines and anthologies. Her longer work includes the novels, *The Five Turns of the Wheel* and *Reborn*, and the novellas, *Bottled* and *Paused*. Her novel, *The Woodcutter*, is due for release via Brigids Gate Press in 2023. Her dark poetry has been published in her collections *Foundlings* (co-authored with Cindy O'Quinn), *Lilith Rising* (co-authored with Shane Douglas Keene) and *Metallurgy*, as well as the *HWA Poetry Showcase Volumes VI, VII, VIII and IX*. She can be found supporting indie authors at HorrorTree.com via the weekly Indie Bookshelf Releases. She is an active member of the HWA and can be found at stephanieellis.org, on Twitter at @el_stevie, Instagram @stephanieellis7963 and also somewhere on Facebook.

ROSS JEFFERY

Ross is the Bram Stoker Award-nominated and 3x Splatterpunk Award-nominated author of *Tome, Juniper, Scorched, Only The Stains Remain, Milk Kisses & Other stories, Beautiful Atrocities* and *Tethered*. He has been published in print with a number of anthologies and his short fiction has also appeared in various online journals. Ross' work has also been translated into other languages. Ross lives in Bristol with his wife (Anna) and two children (Eva and Sophie). You can follow him on Twitter @RossJeffery_

R. J. JOSEPH

R. J. Joseph is a Stoker Award™ nominated, Texas based writer who earned her MFA in Writing Popular Fiction from Seton Hill University and who must exorcise the demons of her imagination so they don't haunt her being. A lifelong horror fan and writer of many things, she joyously discovered and embraced writing in the academic arena about three important aspects of her life: horror, Black femininity, and popular culture. She has had works published in various venues, including the Halloween issue of *Southwest Review* and *The Streaming of Hill House: Essays on the Haunting Netflix Series*. When R. J. isn't writing, teaching, or reading voraciously, she can usually be found wrangling one of various sprouts or sproutlings from her blended family of 11...along with one husband and one hellbeast that masquerades as a dog sometimes. R.J. is also an instructor at The Speculative Fiction Academy and a co-host of the Genre Blackademia podcast. R. J. can be found lurking (and occasionally even peeking out) on Twitter @rjacksonjoseph

RAYNE KING

Rayne King is an author of horror and dark fiction, with several short stories and the novella, *The Creek*, to his name. As an autodidact, he has learned to write through trial and tribulation. His influences are widespread, ranging from magical realism to cosmic horror. Because of this, his writing borrows elements from a multitude of genres, as he feels comfortable using whatever tools necessary to tell his sinister tales. He resides in the Hudson Valley with his family. Find him on Twitter @Channel_King.

BRENNAN LAFARO

Brennan LaFaro is a horror writer living in southeastern Massachusetts with his wife, two sons, and his hounds. An avid lifelong reader, Brennan also co-hosts the *Dead Headspace* podcast. Brennan is the author of *Noose*, the *Slattery Falls* trilogy, *Last Stay*, and *Illusions of Isolation*. You can read his short fiction in various anthologies and find him on Twitter at @brennanlafaro or at brennanlafaro.com. Subscribe to his monthly newsletter at brennanlafaro.substack.com.

TIM MEYER

Tim dwells in a dark cave near the Jersey Shore. He's the author of more than fifteen novels, including *Malignant Summer, The Switch House, Dead Daughters, Limbs,* and many other titles. When he's not working on the next book, he's usually hanging out with his wife and son, shooting around on the basketball court, playing video games, or messing with a new screenplay. He bleeds coffee and IPAs.

MO MOSHATY

Mo is an Afro-Latina screenwriter, author and producer. Raised within the clash of her mother's Yaqui heritage and her father's strict Southern Baptist upbringing, Mo's work contains worlds in which characters of color strive for identity, sentiment and belonging within the comedy, horror, and sci-fi genres. Never shying away from taboo subjects, Mo's award-winning sex comedy pilot, *Catch* earned her a seat in the prestigious 2022 WGI Support Staff Training Program, graduating from the Script Coordinator Track. Co-founder of the Nyx Horror Collective, she's partnered with Stowe Story Labs to provide a fellowship for women genre writers over 40, and has also partnered with horror streaming giant, Shudder, to co-produce the 13 Minutes of Horror Film Festival 2021 and 2022. Still engaging with her first love, short horror literature, her work can be found in *A Quaint and Curious Volume of Gothic Tales*, by Brigid's Gate Press and *206 Word Stories* by Bag O' Bones Press.

BRET NELSON

Bret is an Emmy-award-winning creator. He's worked with Kermit the Frog and John Crichton. Mickey Mouse and Buzz Lightyear, too. He makes TV programs, movies, and stage shows. Plus, video and tabletop games. And TOYS. Right now, he's working on things he can't talk about (that's what the contracts say).

MOCHA PENNINGTON

Mocha studied Journalism with a minor in creative writing at UCM. She separates her time writing and co-hosting *Tea Time*, a gossip channel on YouTube.

STEPHANIE RABIG

Stephanie is the author of *On Stolen Land, Playing Possum*, and the *Cryptids & Cauldrons* series. Her short fiction can be found in *Diet Riot, Slash-Her, Monstroddities, Santa Claws is Coming to Deathlehem*, and *Shiver*. When not writing, she's making resin art, wading through her TBR list, or chasing after her cats.

JUDITH SONNET

Judith (She/Her) is an extreme horror author. Her books are disturbing, dark, and disgusting. When she's not writing horror, she's cuddling her pet cat and watching old slasher movies on

VHS. She's a trans woman and a lesbian. Her titles include *Torture the Sinners!, For the Sake Of, The Clown Hunt* and an erotic novella called *Greta's Fruitcup*. She lives in the Midwest. She can be reached on Instagram—@fulltimehorrorjunkie—where she is usually writing and posting about her favorite books and movies.

MARKUS J. WILLIAMS

Markus is a poet, painter and writer, who also dabbles in photography, videography and composing. He resides in Sacramento, California with his partner and their two cats.

KEN WINKLER

Ken is the co-writer, producer, and director of the award-winning horror feature *Kiss the Abyss*, and recently released his first book, *Old Dread No. 9*, through Encyclopocalypse Publications. He lives with his wife and rescue pup in Southern California.

ABOUT THE EDITOR

JANINE PIPE

Trading in a police badge and then classroom, Janine is a full-time Splatterpunk Award nominated author and editor with Encyclopalypse Publications. She is also a director and producer with Pipe Screams Productions whilst juggling being a mum, wife and Disney addict. A lot of coffee is involved. Influenced by the works of King from a young age, she likes to shock readers with violence and scare them with monsters - both mythical and man-made. Her biggest fans are her loving husband and daughter. And the dog. Follow her on Twitter @janinepipe28

ABOUT ENYCLOPOCALYPSE PUBLICATIONS

Encyclopocalypse was founded as a place where books can live on. From independent novels to literature published before the digital age, our goal is to create a home for every great book that hasn't yet been heard.

PRESIDENT - MARK ALAN MILLER

Mark is an award-winning producer and New York Times Bestselling author. He has written and produced dozens of titles across high-level outlets. He's developed and created content with Clive Barker, Tom Holland, Joe R. Lansdale, Dark Horse Comics, Boom Studios, and St. Martin's Press. He is the Founder and President of Encyclopocalypse Publications, which boasts top-tier clientele and titles across all genres. Mark has represented, organized, developed, and produced hundreds of hours of content, that have grossed millions of dollars for his clients and collaborators.

MANAGING EDITOR - SEAN DUREGGER

Sean is an award-winning audiobook narrator with a lifelong love for horror, sci-fi, fantasy, and cinema trash. He lives in Southern California with his wife, three kids, and two dogs, and is the only one of the team who understands anything about the internet.

facebook.com/encyclopocalypsepub

twitter.com/EnPocalypsePub

instagram.com/encyclopocalypsepub